MAIA *and* ATLAS

by

JAMES A. PEREZ

BARROW COURT BOOKS

HUNTINGTON, NEW YORK

For Jordi, hero in the making

CONTENTS

A noiseless patient spider,
I mark'd where on a little promontory it stood isolated,
Mark'd how to explore the vacant vast surrounding,
It launch'd forth filament, filament, filament, out of itself,
Ever unreeling them, ever tirelessly speeding them.

And you O my soul where you stand,
Surrounded, detached, in measureless oceans of space,
Ceaselessly musing, venturing, throwing,
seeking the spheres to connect them,
Till the bridge you will need be form'd,
till the ductile anchor hold,
Till the gossamer thread you fling catch somewhere,
O my soul.

Walt Whitman (1819 – 1892)

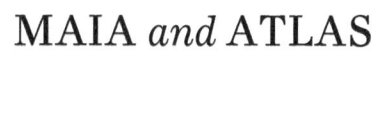

MAIA *and* ATLAS

PROLOGUE

THE CREATURE'S THIRST

A 'TWEEN BOY, YEARS AWAY from being able to shave, pushed his way through the crowd gathered in the Plateia Varkiza. The air was pungent with wine and cologne with hints of lavender and cigarette smoke. Like a rabbit on the lam, the boy ducked and weaved, knocking into several people enjoying the cool breeze drifting up from the beach. The boy avoided an elbow to his temple by edging up against a pair of men swearing and gesticulating about their team's loss in a soccer match. The shorter of the men cursed as his shoes were saturated with beer spilled by his companion. Wiping perspiration from his brow, the boy ran up to a girl with hair the color of coal sitting with a group of teenagers on a wall made of jagged stones. He clapped his hands, and the girl peered at him, drumming her finely manicured fingertips on her leg.

"What is it now?"

The boy cupped a sweaty hand to the girl's ear. She flinched but allowed him to deliver his message.

"Oh, please! You can tell Giorgos he's wasting his time," the girl shouted over the music echoing through the plaza. "Go!"

The boy stumbled over an uneven slab of cement in the ground and dove back into the crowd to deliver the message. The girl turned to one of her friends and narrowed her eyes. Her friend tossed her hair back and laughed, and the girl grinned, tipping her palms up.

The sound of the chaotic scene filling the square reverberated down the adjacent streets. Past a pharmacy flashing with a neon green cross, the music was lost over the low growl of a creature with the body of a man and the head of a ram lumbering in an alley. The beast lapped up water from a puddle formed by condensation dripping from an air conditioner several stories above. Licking its lips, the creature cocked its head in the direction of the opening of the alley.

"*GGGGGRRRRRR!*"

The squalid water failed to satisfy the creature's thirst. It craved blood. The abomination lurched forward only to fall on its face. It pawed at the collar and chain keeping it from its prey.

"Not yet, beastie. Soon we will have the one the mistress seeks," said a bearded man with red eyes. He pulled at the chain, and the creature reached to take another drink.

Back in the square, the dark-haired girl stood and straightened her cut-off denim shorts. She waved at her friends and sidled past the masses, slinking through a crowded café before emerging onto the sidewalk.

"Helena! Where are you going?" called her friend. "We just got here."

"Yes, and I am already tired of Giorgos's nonsense. The boys in this town are just that – boys!" Helena hissed over her shoulder as she glided down the sidewalk. Her friend ran after her and grabbed Helena's arm as she passed under the neon green pharmacy sign.

"Helena, please don't go!"

Helena slapped her friend's arm away. "Let go of me. You can stay, but I am so bored I could die."

The creature lunged forth from the alley, its claws cutting into Helena's leg. Spinning, Helena fell backward onto the pavement.

Her friend reached for her, only to be grabbed by the creature and pulled into the alley.

Over the blood-curdling scream of her friend, Helena scrambled to her feet.

"*AIEEE!*"

She looked at the gaping wound on her calf and fell to her knees. As Helena lost consciousness, the screams from the alley stopped.

CHAPTER ONE

GRADUATION DAY

"MAIA PETERSON."

Take the diploma with your left hand, shake with your right hand, Maia repeated. She straightened her cranberry-colored graduation gown and stepped forward.

"Congratulations, Maia!"

"Thanks, Mr. Foster!"

Maia's guidance counselor squeezed her hand. She looked at Mr. Foster for a moment and then reached out to embrace him. "Thanks for everything," she said softly.

Mr. Foster pulled back and smiled at Maia. "You're welcome. Good luck!"

Crossing the makeshift stage erected for graduation, Maia turned to the crowd of parents and other loved ones seated in white plastic folding chairs on the football field of Sea Cliff High School. After a moment of searching, she recognized her father's mop of curly brown hair. Maia's mother was not anywhere to be seen. Her father, Matthias, seemed to recognize the uncertainty on Maia's face and gestured to the top of the bleachers. Maia's mother, Eleanor, waved to her with one hand, while the other held the hand of Maia's one-year-old brother, Jordi.

Maia stepped down from the stage and walked to the end of her row. As she made her way to her seat, she passed her best friend, Jackie Tan, who sat on the edge of her chair as she waited to be called.

"Great speech, Jackie!"

"Really? Thanks! I was so sure I was going to blow it," Jackie said, biting her bottom lip.

"You sounded awesome. It was the best valedictorian speech today."

"It was the only valedictorian speech today," Jackie countered.

"Still... "

Maia took her seat. To her left, a boy was trying to blow up a beach ball covered in marker with curses under his robe. Maia scratched at her eyebrow. There were some things about high school she wasn't going to miss. She craned her neck to see the bleachers. Maia's mother and brother were climbing down the steps.

Maia's lips curled into a smile as she watched her mother scoop Jordi up and walk to where her father was seated. Jordi squealed with laughter as Maia's father grabbed him into his arms. Her mother looked over and waved before taking a seat next to her father.

It had been a remarkable two years since Maia's father had reentered her life. Her parents took little time getting to know each other again. Jordi was born almost nine months to the day after they were reunited in the lobby of the Royal Olympic Hotel in Athens, Greece. In a short span of time, Maia's family had doubled in size, and she couldn't be more content.

"JORDAN RUBIN."

The graduates in Jackie's row stood up. Her best friend had been with Maia in Greece on the day her parents were brought back together, but Jackie remembered little of it, having been distracted by a boy named Roc from a Spanish youth ambassador group. Despite the distance between Sea Cliff, New York and

Barcelona, Spain, Jackie and Roc were still going strong, with their own reunion planned for later in the summer.

"Hey, MVP," whispered the girl next to Maia, "are you going to Jackson's party at the yacht club?"

"Nah, I don't think so. My folks want to take me out to dinner."

"So, come after dinner," the girl said. "The party is going to go on all night. His parents rented out the whole place. It's going to be epic."

"We'll see how... " Maia began, but the girl had already turned around and was asking the boy next to her the same question. Maia could think of few things less appealing than a drunken graduation party. It wasn't that she didn't fit in with her peers or thought herself better than them, but their worldview was much narrower. Maia had not only been to Greece; she'd been to a hidden world called Olympia, populated by people and creatures only seen in books or films recounting the tales of Greek mythology. That's where her father, once the Titan known as Atlas, had been for most of Maia's life, kept prisoner by Zeus, king of the gods of Olympus. But Maia had rescued her father from an eternity shouldering the heavens and in the process had been inducted into the fierce sisterhood known as the Amazons. She'd also killed Heracles, the son of Zeus, but she preferred not to linger on that thought.

"JACKIE TAN."

"Yeah, Jackie!" Maia cried. Jackie squealed, waving her diploma like a baton. Maia watched Jackie's eyes turn toward the crowd. Mr. and Mrs. Tan were seated not far from Maia's parents, along with Jackie's two brothers. Zack was in college, and Sam went to a special school for children with autism.

Maia knew it was because of Sam that Jackie had decided to study to become a medical doctor. She admired Jackie for realizing how she wanted to make her mark on this world because she still had no clue. Well, at least not on *this* world.

* * *

MAIA TOSSED HER CAP and gown onto her bed.

Clink!

An object bounced off the bed and hit the floor. She bent down and picked up her pin from the Music Honor Society. Maia held the G clef-shaped trinket in her hand. Receiving it had been a surprise, considering how little effort she'd put into band over the last two years. Maia had contemplated dropping out more than once, but let the thought go when she recalled how much music had meant to her grandfather. Her bedroom had been his, and it'd been empty for the time between Grandpa's death and Jordi's birth when Maia switched to the bigger room. It was another change that'd taken some getting used to since her father's return, but hardly the biggest.

"Hey," said Maia's mother, poking her head in the doorway. "I got Jordi down for a nap. We'll go out when he wakes, okay?"

"Sure, Mom, no problem."

"Jackie gave a good speech today. Her mom was crying the whole time," Eleanor said as she entered the room.

"Oh, I didn't think you got to hear it. I figured you were chasing Jordi around."

"No, it was your father's turn at that point. Your friend is going to do amazing things, starting at Harvard this fall."

Maia sat down on the edge of her bed, and her mother joined her. "She was really nervous, but I don't think it showed."

"Not at all," Eleanor agreed. "Just like you out on the field – cool as ice."

"Which field?" Maia asked.

"Well, I'd have to say the lacrosse field, since that's the only field I've seen you on." Her mother stood, folding her arms. "Maia, I don't think I want to go down this path again."

"I know, Mom. I'm sorry. It's just that we never talk about it. You bring up where Jackie is going to college, but—"

"But I don't talk about your plans. Or, I should say, the plans you and father discuss when I'm not around or you're down in the basement in mock combat."

"Mom, that's not fair. We would, that is, I would talk to you about what I'd like to do, but you never give me the chance."

"Battlefield."

"What?" Maia asked.

"A battlefield, right? That's the other 'field' you were referring to," said Maia's mother. "Maia, I accept your *experiences* in Olympia, but that doesn't mean I want them to continue. You were almost killed – more than once."

"It's not just about my experiences there. It's about who I am. And who Dad is. In any event, I wasn't talking about a battlefield."

"Then what kind of 'field' did you mean?"

"I don't know. It was a stupid thing to say, okay? It's just that I don't know what to feel about today. Graduation is supposed to be a celebration, but all I could think about was finally getting out of here. I'm sorry if that hurts you, but it's true. Other than you and Dad getting back together and Jordi being born, there's nothing in the last two years that compares to what happened to me in Olympia."

Maia's mother grabbed her by the hand. "Don't you think I know that? Sweetie, I've had to come to terms with a lot of things in the last couple of years, too. Being married to, you know, a

Titan. My husband is the guy they actually named atlases after. So, give me some credit."

"Mom... "

"But the hardest thing, after we got home, was seeing how... different you were and knowing that I could never fully understand what you'd been through," said Eleanor, tears welling. "As your mother, that tore me up in ways you'll never understand until you're a parent. I know how difficult it's been for you. And I know that nothing you experience in *this* world is ever going to feel the same as it would for someone else your age."

From the other side of the wall came a plaintive *"WAAAAAAAH!"*

"Your brother's awake," said Maia's mother as she leaned in and kissed her on the forehead.

"Mom, I'm sorry—"

"It's fine, Maia. We'll talk more later."

Maia fell back on her bed. That'd been a disaster. Maia jerked her neck – she'd landed on something hard. Sitting up, she yanked her graduation gown away. Lying in the middle of her bed was a small leather-bound book with decorative gold tooling.

"What the hell?"

Maia reached for the book when a sharp pain flared on her wrist where she wore a gold bracelet given to her by Zeus. *"AHH!"* she cried, pulling back her hand. The book began to shake and then flew open with an explosion of light and smoke, knocking Maia to the floor. Her bedroom door slammed shut.

"THE BARRIER WILL FALL!" boomed a voice from the book itself. "AND YOU WITH IT!"

The voice was familiar. "Akantha?" Maia asked, shielding her eyes.

"Maia! What is it? What's going on?" her mother yelled from the hallway.

"Maia, are you alright?" shouted her father from the bottom of the stairs.

"YOU WILL NOT ESCAPE THE FALL OF OLYMPIA! SEEK OUT YOUR COUSIN!"

The book spun in the air to the sound of laughter and fell upon Maia's bed, where it crumbled to dust. Her father broke the bedroom door down and slid to his knees next to Maia.

"What happened? Are you okay?" Matthias asked as he pulled her into his arms.

Maia's mother rushed into the room holding a crying Jordi. "My god, what was that?"

Maia covered her bracelet with her hand. "It was a graduation present."

CHAPTER TWO

ANOTHER SYMBOL

ELEANOR HUNG UP THE TELEPHONE. "The food will be here in twenty minutes. This isn't exactly what we had in mind to celebrate your graduation, but under the circumstances... "

"It's fine," Maia said. "I'm not hungry anyway."

"You better be. You can't let your father eat all of the egg rolls by himself," her mother said, sitting next to Maia at their kitchen table. "How are you feeling?"

"I'm okay," Maia lied. She rested her head on her mother's shoulder. "I'm sorry about before. I shouldn't have—"

"Maia, stop. We have plenty of time to talk about the past. Right now, we have to figure out what to do in the present."

Eleanor put her arm around her daughter. Maia met her eyes and smiled. Her mother, their earlier argument aside, was remarkably understanding. Maia moved to hug her, knocking a stack of mail onto the floor. She reached over and picked up a coupon book, guitar magazine, and a letter. Maia dropped the coupon book and magazine upon closer look at the letter.

"Did this come today?" Maia asked, squeezing the letter tightly enough to crumple it.

"I guess so. Your father must've brought it in while we were upstairs. What's wrong?"

"It's the letter I wrote to Nate." Maia swallowed after saying the name of her first kiss.

"The boy from the youth ambassador program you met in Greece? He wrote you back?" Eleanor asked.

"No. It's *my* letter. 'Return to sender.' Just like the last two I sent him," Maia said, tearing the letter in half.

"Easy there, Maia. Isn't his mother in the military? Maybe they moved again."

"With no forwarding address?" Maia shook her head. She'd never gotten a straight answer out of Nate about a curious comment he'd made shortly after meeting him in Greece. He'd denied having knowledge of Olympia, but that didn't stop Maia from believing Nate was keeping secrets, especially after he'd disappeared a few months ago.

A creaking noise traveled down the stairs. A moment later, Maia's father walked into the kitchen wearing a sleeveless white t-shirt with a faint trace of vomit.

"Jordi give you a hard time?"

"He cried until he, well... " Matthias recounted, pointing to his shirt. "But he is finally asleep. Did you order dinner?"

Maia laughed. "You've got puke on your shirt, and you're still thinking about food?"

"There is always time to eat, Maia. Especially when everything else is uncertain."

"Oh boy, there you go," said Eleanor.

"What?"

"Don't say things like that. Not until we know what's going on."

"That is my point – we don't know what's certain. Now, Maia, where did the leather book come from?"

"It looks like one that Jackie's brother gave me two years ago. Zack found it in his car after he gave me a ride. He thought it was mine. Anyway, it disappeared not long after."

"Disappeared?"

"The last time I remember seeing it was when I was packing for Greece. I thought about bringing it, but I left it on my desk. I couldn't read it. It was written in Greek. It wasn't there when we got back. To be honest, I never gave it a second thought after that."

"Was there anything else about it you can remember?" Eleanor asked.

Maia crossed the kitchen and looked through the window to her backyard. She pictured herself opening the book after Zack had given it to her. There *was* something else. "Yes! There was a piece of paper inside. It was a drawing of a girl. She was holding a sword that looked a lot like the symbol of the sword on my bracelet." Maia turned her hand over. "*Oh!* There's a new symbol!"

"What is it?" her father asked. "Did it just show up?"

"It's a snake, I think. It wasn't there this morning. It must've shown up after the book exploded."

Matthias twisted Maia's bracelet over and again, his brow furrowed. He looked at Maia's mother and gave her a weak smile.

"Matt, what is it?"

"I do not believe it's a snake, at least not a normal one. It looks like an amphisbaena. It's a creature from Olympia – a serpent with two heads, sometimes with feet." Her father held Maia's hands in his. "What else can you remember about before? You said the voice was familiar."

"Yes, it sounded like Akantha, King Alphaios's daughter, but I don't know how that's possible," said Maia. "The last time I saw her was during the battle between Heracles's army and the Amazons. She was dragged off by a gryphon." Maia smirked as she recalled the terrified look on Akantha's face as the spoiled princess and traitor to the Amazons, as well as Maia's self-described archenemy, was seized by the talons of a ferocious creature part lion and part eagle. "Even if she survived, she'd lost everything.

Her father was dead, and the Amazons would never take her back. It's not like she had... oh, wait a minute! Akantha spoke of a mother. She said her mother gave her the human-animal hybrids that fought the Amazons."

"You told me this before, Maia, but I failed to consider the implications," said Matthias. "There is only one person in Olympia capable of creating such beasts. Yet I did not know her to have a daughter. She actually helped me when I first left Olympia."

"Who is she, Matt?" asked Eleanor.

"Her name is Circe, and she was quite a powerful witch." Matthias closed his eyes. "I had no reason to give her much thought after I was freed from Zeus's imprisonment in the garden of the Hesperides."

"Matt, I'm sorry. I know all of this is important, but don't you think we should call Dorian? Nothing like this has occurred in two years. Your brother will know what's happening in Olympia. There are too many peculiarities. First the book, and then the symbol on Maia's bracelet."

"The voice said, 'Seek out your cousin,' right before the book fell. Could she be talking about Helena? Mom's right, we have to call Uncle Dorian. What if—"

RING!

Maia and her parents looked back and forth between each other. Tightening her lips, Maia crossed the kitchen to where the telephone hung on the wall.

RING!

"Maia, answer the phone!"

Maia grabbed the receiver. Her words caught in her throat. "He-Hello?"

"Thank Zeus you are alive!"

"Uncle Dorian, we were just going to call you. Something unbelievable just happened."

"And here as well. There has been a breach of the barrier that separates this world from Olympia."

"Uncle Dorian, let me put the speaker phone on so Mom and Dad can hear you. Hang on a second."

"Can you all hear me?" asked Dorian.

"Yes, brother. Eleanor and I wish to know what you've shared with Maia," said Matthias.

"Our niece Helena was attacked. She survived, but is barely clinging to life. A friend was not so fortunate. By all accounts, it was a creature half-man, half-beast. Needless to say, I am afraid you are all in grave danger."

"Have you journeyed to Olympia, brother? We must know what has taken place to allow for such an assault to occur."

"Yes, Matthias, I agree. I needed to alert you first. But what has happened in Sea Cliff?" Dorian asked. "There are no coincidences where Olympia is involved."

Maia quickly related the incident with the book, as well as the appearance of a new symbol on her bracelet.

"Dorian, how quickly can you travel to Olympia?"

There was no answer.

"Dorian, are you there?"

After several seconds, Dorian answered. "I am here, brother. Only I am more worried than before. There were rumors that Circe had grown in power after the death of Zeus, but I did not think she was capable of engineering an attack in this world. The book does sound like one of her devices, though. If it is, then it means she has been plotting since before you were freed."

Maia was surprised by the fear in her uncle's voice. After all, like her father, Dorian hadn't always been human. Before the creation of Olympia, he was Poseidon, god of the sea. Maia was equally dismayed by the worry on her father's face. How were the machinations of a witch striking fear in both a dethroned god of Olympus and a former Titan?

"Brother, I would journey to Olympia with you, but—"

"No, Matthias, you need to be by your family's side. I will prepare to go once I am certain Helena is out of danger."

"How is Hera?"

"Our dear 'mother' remains as muddled as always. It is better that way. Helena's father has been a raging ass."

"*Ugh!* I never liked that guy," Maia said, though she regretted her admission almost immediately. Helena's father was gruff and obnoxious, but Maia could only imagine his pain at seeing his daughter suffer. When Jordi was six months old, he contracted meningitis and spent a week in the hospital. Her recollection of the distress of her parents was enough to make her feel compassion for Helena's father – even if he was indeed an ass.

"Dorian, is there any way to keep someone else from crossing over from Olympia?" Maia's mother asked, her voice trembling. Matthias held his wife in his arms.

"Not that I am aware, but your question does strengthen my resolve to seek out one who may be able to make that come to pass," Dorian answered. "Just a moment." A muffled sound came from the telephone. "Helena has awoken. I must go."

"Of course, brother. Call us when you can."

"Dad, who was Uncle Dorian talking about? Who could affect the barrier, unless... oh, no! If it's who I'm thinking of, he makes Helena's father look like the Easter Bunny."

"Who is it?" Eleanor asked.

"The artificer known as Daedalus," said Maia's father.

"Maia, didn't you know his son?"

"Yes. His name was Icarus. And he was there when this whole mess got started."

CHAPTER THREE

AN UNEXPECTED REUNION

MAIA ROLLED ACROSS THE FLOOR and threw her spear at a large target, sticking it in the bull's eye. She grabbed her bow, loaded an arrow, and struck the center of another smaller target. Standing, Maia unsheathed her sword and charged a dummy perched between the targets. She came within a foot of piercing the dummy's face, but instead slid to her knees and kicked the dummy's legs out from under it. Back on her feet, Maia jabbed the dummy in the face with her sword before placing the weapon back in its sheath. She pulled her spear from the target and spun around, ducking and weaving from an imaginary opponent. Maia crossed the entirety of the large warehouse this way, before finally using the spear as an aid to vault onto a pile of wood pallets. She pulled back the spear and launched it across the warehouse, splitting the arrow in the smaller target from nock to tip.

Maia jumped down from the pallets. She grabbed a towel and a bottle of water from a nearby folding chair. Her footsteps echoed through the empty warehouse as she approached the targets. Maia picked up the dummy and put it on its feet. She straightened the white t-shirt the dummy wore, across which Maia had written 'AKANTHA.' With the speed of a hummingbird's wings, Maia stabbed the dummy through the chest with her sword.

"Another dummy bites the dust," said Maia's father from a catwalk. "Thank you for not beheading it. They are rather expensive."

"It was tempting," Maia said, once again sheathing her sword. She chugged the remains of her water and draped the towel around her neck. "I didn't think you were coming."

"It started to rain. There was not much reason to stay at the construction site," Matthias responded as he descended a metal stairway to the warehouse floor. "I like your graffiti," he added, motioning to the dummy.

"I thought I could use some inspiration."

"And did you?"

"Turns out not so much. I'm ready to take on a herd of gryphons," said Maia, hitting the dummy in the head with the empty water bottle. "Or whatever you call a pack of amphisbaenas."

"*Ha!* Queen Hippolyta would be proud. This warehouse was a good find," said Matthias, surveying the space. "It's been vacant for a few years. I am thinking of putting in an offer to purchase it instead of continuing to lease."

"Peterson Construction and Development is doing pretty well, I guess," said Maia. "Grandpa would be proud, too."

"I hope so. I am sorry that I never met your grandparents, especially your grandfather. From tales your mother tells, I would imagine he could outdrink Dionysus. And he was a shrewd businessman. If he had not had to slow things down after your grandmother took sick, your grandfather could have grown his one-man building firm into something much bigger. I am proud to have taken the appellation Peterson."

"It wasn't the first time you've changed names."

"Indeed."

"Well, this is definitely a better space to train than our basement. Remember when we broke the boiler?" asked Maia. "I thought Mom was going to pick up a sword and—"

"In her defense, she was eight months pregnant and not in the best of humor."

"*Ha!* Anyway, that's enough chit chat. Are you ready to spar?"

"Haven't you worked out enough for one day?" asked Matthias, raising his eyebrows.

"Given the circumstances, I think we both need to be at the top of our games."

"So be it, Maia. But do not go crying to your mother when I beat my own record for how quickly I can disarm you."

"Big talk," said Maia. "Go suit up."

* * *

MAIA KICKED HER FATHER'S SWORD out of his reach. Matthias lay on his back clutching his side. Maia grabbed a towel and threw it at her father.

"Thank you for going easy on your old man," he said. "*Argh!* I think you broke a rib. *Hmmm. Hmmm-huh. Ha ha ha ha haah!*"

"Did I hit your head? Why are you laughing?"

"Because it is preferable to crying. You will see when you are my age," answered her father.

"Aren't you like 10,000 years old?"

"I lost count when I was holding the sky on my shoulders for a few millennia." Matthias heaved himself to his feet. "*Aaaaarrr!* That's going to hurt for a while. No horsey rides for your brother this evening."

"Seriously, are you okay?"

"Yes, Maia, I am fine. More than fine, actually. All of your practicing has paid off. Your skills are quite impressive. Though I still hope you will not need them."

Maia sat crisscross on the floor. "Yeah, about that. Dad, I want to—"

"There is no need to finish that sentence. I know what you are going to say."

"Even if we weren't on high alert after that book showed up or Helena was attacked, I was going back to Olympia," Maia said, locking eyes with her father. Her heartbeat pounded in her ears. Maia had been holding onto the admission of her plans for such a long time that she'd thought of little else. She watched her father for a reaction, counting each inhalation and exhalation.

"Thank you for finally putting that out there, Maia," said her father after several seconds. "I have been waiting for a while. Luckily, I learned to be patient a long time ago."

"Are you angry?" Maia asked.

"No. Being mad at you for desiring to return to Olympia would be like being angry at the sun for wanting to rise. I cannot fight what is your clear destiny, and neither can your mother. She told me about your quarrel after graduation. It pains her tremendously to think of you being in harm's way, but she knows better than to try to stop what has already been set in motion," said Matthias, arching his back. "All we ask is that you wait to hear back from Dorian."

Maia blinked back tears as she jumped into her father's arms. "Thank you," she whispered. Maia rested her head on her father's chest as he bowed his head and kissed her on top of her sweaty, bushy mane of hair.

"*Ah ah ah ah!* Don't squeeze too hard," said her father, tittering with laughter. "And you are stabbing me in the knee with your sword."

"Sorry!" Maia cried as she undid her belt, allowing her scabbard to fall to the ground.

"*Ooof!* All right, well, grab your things. We've been at this for almost two hours. And it's 'Taco Tuesday!' It doesn't get much better than that."

"*Ha!* Mom does make a mean taco. If it's okay I'm going to walk home," said Maia. "You go. I'll lock everything away."

"You can walk, but I'll take care of this mess. We will call it my 'cool down.' I'll see you at home," Matthias said, tossing his towel at Maia.

"I love you, Dad."

"Not as much as I love you."

Maia picked up a hooded sweatshirt and pulled it over her head as she climbed the stairs to the catwalk and out the door. The warehouse was located in the neighboring town of Glenwood Landing, and Maia was grateful for the long walk home. After a few turns, she emerged on a hill overlooking Hempstead Harbor. The sun would be setting in an hour or so, and Maia quivered with delight as she decided to make a stop before heading home. She walked along a busy tree-lined street across from Tappen Beach. Camp counselors in red polo shirts were putting away athletic equipment. A group of children chased each other on the beach while their parents yelled at them not to kick sand, warning them (half-heartedly) that they were going home.

Maia came to the end of the beach and continued walking up a hill toward the village center of Sea Cliff. She saw a street sign for Sea Cliff Avenue and quickened her pace. Maia let out a huge breath as she turned into Memorial Park at the intersection of Prospect and Sea Cliff Avenues. Sometimes called "Sunset Park" or "Hippie Park" by the locals, Maia thought of it as just about her favorite place – in *any* world. Wiping away any remaining traces of the earlier rain, Maia sat on a bench, as she'd done countless times before, and looked out at the harbor. Immediately, her breathing slowed and her muscles, though sore from hours of mock combat, relaxed. Maia closed her eyes, taking solace in the rich memories she held of Memorial Park. She'd spent many an afternoon there reading books with her mother or listening to Jackie worry about a test on which she'd later receive a perfect score. It was in this park, as well, that Maia had her first inkling that there may be a world outside of the one she knew, when she spied the sea god Triton out in the harbor. And it was on the same bench that Maia's mother had shared the circumstances of Maia's birth and her father's disappearance – at least from her mother's perspective.

The snapping of a branch interrupted the quiet, signaling that Maia wasn't alone in the park. She filled her lungs deeply once more and opened her eyes.

"Hello, Maia," said a most unexpected voice.

Maia kept her eyes forward, her arms riddled with goose bumps and her toes curled in her sneakers. She gripped the arm of the bench and turned in her seat to face her company.

""I guess I should be surprised, but I'm not," said Maia. "Hello, Icarus."

CHAPTER FOUR

THE STRENGTH OF A TITAN

A ROOT BEER COLORED MUSTANG CONVERTIBLE came to a screeching halt at a stop sign on Prospect Avenue, barely missing a black Escalade as it turned off Sea Cliff Avenue. The driver, a teenage girl, and her two female passengers laughed uncontrollably at their near accident before speeding down the hill. Seconds later, a car horn sounded along with the din of grinding brakes.

"Fascinating," said Icarus, his attention turned to a screaming match occurring down the road.

"Irresponsible, I would call it. And a waste of their promise," said Maia. "Captain Penelopeia would have throttled them."

"Ah, yes. The Amazons have high expectations for all those of their gender. Congratulations on your acceptance into their nation," said Icarus.

"Thank you. Congratulations on being alive."

"Maia, I can—"

"Stop. Just stop and... " Maia stepped forward and hugged Icarus. "I can't believe you're alive." For the second time that afternoon, Maia's eyes filled with happy tears. Icarus hugged Maia back, at which point her crying continued in earnest.

"I am sorry that I have not come sooner, but my responsibilities in Olympia prevented me from doing so. I am overjoyed to see you, Maia. And I know that I have much to explain."

SCREEEEEECH!

The girls in the Mustang convertible came barreling backwards up the hill on Prospect Avenue, followed by a forward-driving cobalt blue Chevy pickup truck.

"Look out!" screamed a woman crossing the street into Memorial Park with her Yorkshire terrier. The driver of the Mustang swerved backwards onto Sea Cliff Avenue. The man behind the wheel of the truck picked up speed, seeming to aim for the Mustang. The driver of the Mustang threw the car into forward gear and slammed on the gas, jumping the curb and thundering into Memorial Park.

Maia jumped out of the path of the Mustang and knocked Icarus to the ground. The car collided into several benches before coming to a stop at the ledge overlooking the harbor. The driver and her passengers shrieked as the car teetered on the brink. On the street, the driver of the truck cursed and tore away from the scene. Maia scrambled to her feet and ran to the back of the Mustang. She grabbed it by the rear bumper.

"Icarus! Help them out of the car!" Maia yelled, straining to keep a grip on the Mustang. "Just hang on," she shouted at the girls.

"We're going to die!" yelled the driver of the Mustang over the screams of her passengers.

"Shut up and hang on!" Maia hissed.

Icarus edged his way along the side of the car. "Give me your hand," he ordered the girl in the backseat. She continued to scream but didn't move. "Enough! Now, give me your hand!"

Shaking, the girl reached her hand out an inch at a time until Icarus could grab it. The car rocked forward, and the girls let out another volley of screams. Icarus leaned over the rear seat of the car and yanked the girl out by her shoulders. She tumbled to the ground.

"Great!" Maia yelled. "*AAAARRRR!* Get the other two. I can't hold on much longer."

The dirt and trampled shrubbery under the midsection of the Mustang began to crumble, and the car again rocked forward. Icarus grabbed the bumper next to Maia.

"No, you've got to get the girls. I'll hold the car!"

"Just follow my lead," Icarus said as he stepped up onto the trunk of the car. The Mustang slipped forward several inches. Icarus scrambled forward and grabbed the driver and her passenger by their hands. "Maia, take my feet!"

Maia let go of the bumper and held onto Icarus's ankles. The Mustang lurched forward and slid off the edge. Maia pulled back, snatching Icarus and the girls from the car before it plummeted to the wooded area below. The girls continued to shriek as they lay in fetal positions on the ground.

The woman who'd nearly been hit by the Mustang came running forward. "That was amazing! Are you alright?"

Maia pulled the hood of her sweatshirt up over her head. "Go get help," Maia ordered as she sat up. Arching her back, she let out an enthusiastic groan.

"Maia, are you injured?" Icarus asked.

"I'm okay. How about you?"

"Just a few scratches, but otherwise fine. I can not believe—"

"Hold that thought," Maia interrupted. "Let's get out of here."

The three girls had huddled together crying. A hubcap from the Mustang rested next to the remains of Maia's favorite bench. She stepped on the edge of the hubcap, and it popped up into her hand. Maia tossed it next to the girls.

"You're welcome, by the way," Maia said as she took Icarus by the hand. They darted onto the sidewalk leading back to Tappen

Beach. "The fire station is on the other side of town. We'll go a few blocks in this direction before we backtrack to my house."

In the distance, a siren grew louder. Maia quickened her pace, and Icarus followed suit.

"Maia, that was incredible. You have such strength."

"Yeah, well, I guess I take after my dad. Oh, and by the way, when you said my father 'sacrificed' himself, you could've been more precise."

"I could have been more clear about many things. Please accept my apologies. I was far in over my head when I sought you out. I never should have been so bold... or foolish," said Icarus.

Maia crossed the street and ducked through a fence constructed of copper pipes next to a pond. She motioned for Icarus to follow her. "Let's wait here a couple of minutes."

Icarus sat next to Maia on a large rock at the edge of the pond, obscured from the road by a grove of bamboo. A pair of geese swam close to Maia and Icarus.

"Sorry, no food for you two," Maia said. She turned to Icarus. "It wasn't foolish. It was inevitable. I understand that now. But it doesn't mean I wasn't pissed at you for a long time."

"Of course."

"And another thing, your father is a real jerk."

"Also true," said Icarus. "We have been much at odds since my return." Icarus reached into his pocket and pulled out a bracelet – the same bracelet he'd given Maia five years earlier. "I recovered this for you."

"Thank you. Zeus gave me a new one," said Maia, holding up her arm. "How did you find this? I threw it into the sea from the headland of Cape Sounion."

"I have become quite an adept swimmer," said Icarus, his face betraying a storm of emotions. He took Maia by the hand, dropped the bracelet into her palm, and closed her fingers.

"Yeah," Maia said, "I bet you have. So, do I get to hear the story of your return?"

"In time, Maia. We have more important matters to discuss with your father."

"He should be home by now. We can go in a few minutes."

Icarus shifted his position and in doing so revealed a long, deep cut on his arm.

"You weren't kidding about a couple of scratches. Hold my sweatshirt against it."

"I am fine, Maia. The bleeding has stopped. Have you accomplished such feats before?" Icarus asked.

"Yeah, a few, but nothing like that. I've tried to keep a low profile. My best friend, Jackie, tried to convince me to become a superhero."

"What is a 'superhero'?"

"Um, kind of like a god, but with much tighter clothes," Maia said, laughing. "That was crazy, though. I can't believe how phenomenally stupid those girls were."

"Do you worry that you were recognized?" asked Icarus.

"Sea Cliff is a small town, but I didn't know the girls or the woman walking her dog so hopefully they didn't know me. Besides, I don't plan on being here much longer."

"Where will you go?"

"Where do you think?" Maia countered.

"It would not be wise for you to return to Olympia at this time. That is why I have come," said Icarus, "to deliver a message from your uncle."

Maia stood and reached out her hand, pulling Icarus to his feet. She craned her neck around the bamboo. There were no cars on the road, and, while a siren could be heard in the distance, Maia decided that it was safe to move.

"That seems to be the only message my uncle ever wants delivered," said Maia as she stepped through the pipe fence. "We can go up this street."

Icarus stopped and looked back in the direction of Memorial Park. "It is a shame to miss the sunset. Helios, guardian of the sun, does his finest work at the end of the day."

"The day isn't over yet. Besides, there's another Titan who's going to be very interested in what you've to say."

"I must admit that I am somewhat nervous about meeting your father."

"I wouldn't be worried. I mean, he did rip the arms off a doctor who was hassling my mother at work, but he's normally very even tempered."

"You speak in jest," said Icarus.

"*Ha!* Yeah, I'm just kidding," said Maia. "It's my mother you should be scared of meeting."

CHAPTER FIVE

A POWERFUL RESISTANCE

MAIA FUMBLED FOR HER KEYS, patting down the pouch in her hooded sweatshirt and thrusting her hands in and out of her shorts pockets. They weren't to be found. Her keys were probably at the warehouse. Or perhaps they fell out in Memorial Park. Either way, there was no sense retracing her steps. Maia pressed the doorbell.

"Should I remain back?" asked Icarus. "It may be best to keep my presence from your parents for the time being."

"No, no, no. We're not a family that keeps secrets. Well, at least we don't keep secrets anymore. Besides, there isn't much that can surprise my mother these days."

The front door opened. Maia's mother had her hair pulled back and was wearing a white Sea Cliff High School t-shirt with a red stain over the first 'S.' She had a dishrag and a scowl.

"Where've you been? Dad said you'd be home right after him. Oh, hello. Maia, who's this?"

Icarus stepped forward and bowed. "Greetings, mistress of the mighty Atlas. It is an honor to make your acquaintance."

"*Ugh!* Mom, this is Icarus," Maia offered.

"Icarus? As in, Icarus who flew too close to the sun?"

"Yep, that's the one."

"Well, it's nice to meet you, Icarus. But forgive me, aren't you dead?" asked Eleanor.

"Mom!"

"What? I think that's a fair question."

"Fine, but can we come in first before we continue this conversation?" Maia asked, brushing past her mother. "He got... better, okay? Icarus, just come in here."

"Yes, please Icarus. Welcome to our home. Now, if you'll forgive me, I'm not finished cooking dinner. It's 'Taco Tuesday.' I hope you like tacos," said Eleanor before ducking into the kitchen.

"Why, yes, of course," called Icarus. "Tacos are... Maia, what is a taco?"

"You'll like them, trust me. Let's go talk to my father," Maia said. "Did you really just call my mother the 'mistress' of Atlas?"

"She did not seem perturbed," said Icarus.

"Lucky for you. I don't think 'mistress' is a title many women desire."

"Not by my poor choice of words, Maia. Your mother did not seem troubled by my presence, even though she thought me dead."

"She thought my father was dead for fifteen years. I think she's gotten better at rolling with this sort of stuff," offered Maia. "But I'd drop the 'mistress' thing."

"Understood," said Icarus with a nod of his head.

Maia and Icarus passed through the living room to the den, a recent addition to the Peterson home courtesy of Maia's father. Since reuniting with her mother, he'd made several improvements to the house. In the center of the den sat Maia's father with Jordi. A stack of wooden blocks teetered between them.

"Uh oh, the tower's going to fall. Don't let it fall!" roared Matthias to Jordi's great amusement.

Jordi knocked over the blocks with a squeal. Matthias grabbed him up in his arms and tossed him in the air. "You knocked the tower down! Who's going to clean up this mess, *eh*? Not me!"

Jordi shrieked with laughter, especially after his father nudged Jordi's shirt up with his nose and blew a raspberry on his stomach. "Belly trombone!"

It pained Maia to interrupt. "Um, Dad, there's someone you need to meet."

"Maia, when did you get home?" asked Matthias, getting to his feet. "And who's your friend?"

Icarus fell to his knees, his head bowed. "Lord Atlas, it is my great honor to stand before you."

"Oh, brother. Really? By the way, you're kneeling, not standing," said Maia.

"I don't understand," said Maia's father, putting Jordi on a wooden rocking horse with ivory wings.

"I am Icarus, son of Daedalus, and I am your humble servant."

"The son of Daedalus? And back from the dead? Well, actions do have a way of repeating themselves in Olympia," said Matthias. He reached out his hand.

Icarus stared at the former Titan's hand for a moment before shaking it.

"You saved my daughter's life. You have my gratitude." Matthias pulled Icarus in so that barely an inch separated their foreheads. "But you were also the one to endanger her life by first bringing her to Olympia. And for that, you have my scorn."

"My lord, please, I did not mean—"

"*Ha!* Relax, son of Daedalus. I am not in a position to scorn anyone. Besides, Maia would have ended up in Olympia with or without your involvement. That certainty was set in motion long before you were involved. Come! Let us eat tacos. You can explain your presence while we dine." Matthias scooped up Jordi and bounded out of the den to the toddler's fits of laughter.

"That was... unexpected," said Icarus. "I have never seen a deity act in such a manner."

"You'll get used to it."

* * *

ELEANOR HELD A PLATTER under Icarus's nose. "Another taco?"

"No, thank you. I am quite full," said Icarus, patting his stomach. "They were delicious."

"I'm glad you like them."

"As am I," added Matthias. "So, Icarus, tell us why you've come to Sea Cliff."

"I was instructed to do so by the god once known as Poseidon. He had to remain in Olympia."

"Which explains why we haven't heard from him," said Maia. "Mom, can you please pass the guacamole?"

"Actually, Matt, can you pass it?" asked Eleanor as she lifted Jordi from his highchair. "Somebody needs a diaper change," she added as she exited the room.

"What message do you have?"

"Poseidon, that is, Dorian asks that you do not attempt to return to Olympia. It is too dangerous."

Maia dropped her fork. "And what else did he say?"

"There have been more attacks from Olympia. He has surmised that the attacks will continue until there has been restitution."

"To whom?" asked Matthias. "Who is responsible for the attacks?"

"She who is said to sit upon the throne of Lord Zeus. The witch Circe has claimed dominion over the whole of Olympia. And by her side is her daughter Akantha."

"I knew it! Akantha *is* Circe's daughter. And she survived being chewed on by a gryphon," said Maia. "I can't believe she and her mother took over Olympia."

"They have not succeeded in conquering all of the realm. There is a powerful resistance being led by the Amazons and the Argonauts."

"*Ah!* Jason and his band of the mightiest heroes in the history of Greece have joined with Queen Hippolyta. That is an impressive resistance indeed."

"Jason is dead, Lord Atlas. His son now leads the Argonauts. One would think that Circe's forces would be beaten back, but still chaos reigns in Olympia. Circe has used her witchcraft to create a seemingly endless army of mindless, monstrous human-animal hybrids. Dorian is trying to muster other militaries. He went to my father, which is how I came to be here."

"And how is your dear old dad?"

"My father is a great... my father is still an arrogant ass, but he is trying to help Dorian."

"Perhaps I should join him then," said Matthias.

"That's not happening. At least, not without me," countered Maia.

"No! Neither of you are to go," said Icarus. "Forgive my tone, Lord Atlas, but you can not journey to Olympia at this time. We must wait for Dorian's counsel."

Matthias drummed his fingers on the table. "Maia, why don't you take Icarus downstairs. I'll clean up."

Maia pushed back her chair and rocked to her feet. She motioned to Icarus to follow her. Maia opened the door to the basement and flicked on the lights. Icarus followed her down the stairs. At the bottom, Maia pulled down on a rusty pipe and with a loud creak the wall in front of her moved ever so slightly. Maia pushed on the wall until an opening appeared. She directed Icarus to step into the opening and then squeezed in behind him. Maia flipped another switch.

"What is this place?" Icarus asked.

A series of fluorescent lights blinked on one at a time revealing a collection of swords, shields, and wooden staffs amongst other weapons and tools.

"It's our armory. Dad and I've been assembling this for the past two years."

"It is most impressive. But why are you showing me this?"

"Because I can take care of my mother and brother if my father has to go to Olympia. That's why you don't want him to leave. Dorian didn't send you here just to deliver a message. You're supposed to protect us." Maia grabbed a sword and slashed the thick humid air. "We don't need your protection."

"*Hmmm.* You are not the girl I once knew."

"It's been five years. And the last two have been spent getting ready to return to Olympia."

"The Olympia you knew no longer exists," said Icarus as he picked up a shield. "You will need more than just sword skills."

"I've got a lot more than that," said Maia.

"Please," said Icarus as his lips curled up in a goofy grin, "my attention is all yours."

CHAPTER SIX

THE CALL TO BATTLE

MAIA CARRIED A SET OF SHEETS and two pillows down the basement stairs. Icarus sat on the edge of a futon, a bag of frozen peas over his right eye. Maia dropped the sheets and pillows next to Icarus and kneeled in front of him.

"Does it still hurt?" Maia asked, peeking under the bag. "I'm really sorry. I thought you were looking."

"I *was* looking. I watched the entire time as you threw the staff at my head. I was too tired to react," said Icarus.

"*Hmmm.*"

"That is all you have to say?"

"Um... I'm sorry?"

"Yes, you have already apologized. I... I... *Hmmm. Hmmm-huh. Ha ha ha ha – kaff! kaff! – haaah!*"

"*Ha hah ha hah!*" laughed Maia.

"*Ha ha ha!* I do not know why – *ha ha ha!* – I am laughing," said Icarus. "You may have blinded me."

"If it's any consolation, I beat my father this afternoon, too."

"How is that consolation? You already fought a Titan today. You should be exhausted!"

Maia took Icarus by the elbow and directed him to sit on an upside down milk crate. "I'll make your bed. You look like you could use the rest," said Maia. "There's a shower in the bathroom if you want to get washed up before you go to sleep. But you don't have anything to change into."

"I travel light."

"I'll get a t-shirt from my dad. Be right back."

"Take your time. I will not go anywhere."

Maia bounded up the steps through the doorway leading to the kitchen. The only sound was the ticking hand of a cuckoo clock on the wall next to the door. Her parents had gone upstairs with Jordi. Maia crossed the kitchen into the laundry room. She grabbed one of her father's t-shirts out of the dryer along with a pair of boxer shorts. Maia switched off the light in the laundry room as the lights came on in the kitchen.

"Oh, hey Mom. Is Jordi asleep?"

"No, but your dad is – on the floor of Jordi's bedroom. I think Jordi is coloring his face with markers. Are those for Icarus?" Eleanor asked.

"Yeah. You don't think Dad will mind, do you?"

"I'm sure he won't, but Icarus can keep the boxer shorts. How does his eye look? You really have to be more careful. Between Icarus and your father, someone is going to end up in the hospital. Which reminds me – my co-worker Aisha called to tell me a crazy story while you were 'sparring' with Icarus. A car drove through Memorial Park and careened over the side of the ledge. A man and an exceptionally strong woman pulled three girls out of the car before vanishing. The girls were brought to the hospital."

"Are they okay?"

"Thanks to you they are. Were you going to mention this?"

"Are you mad?" asked Maia.

"You think I'm 'mad'? When are you going to stop thinking of me as some shrew? I'm proud of you. I just want to make sure you weren't hurt. And that you weren't recognized."

"I'm fine, Mom. And I covered my head with my hood as soon as it was over."

"Is that supposed to protect your identity? Maybe I should get you a pair of glasses."

"It works for Superman. Anyway, I didn't say anything because I thought dealing with Icarus showing up alive was enough. I'm glad the girls are okay, even though they acted pretty stupid. You should've seen the way they were driving. And they totally destroyed the park!"

"Well, if that's the case, I'm sure the driver isn't going to be behind the wheel of a car anytime soon," said Eleanor. "Maia, what is it?"

"Oh, it's nothing. I just love that park so much."

"So do I, sweetie. I have a lot of good memories of spending time there with you."

Maia hugged her mother. "It's so strange. What's next? Is the library going to burn down?"

"You think every place that's important to you in Sea Cliff is going to disappear just because you've graduated?"

"I'm pretty self-involved, right?"

"That's the last thing I would ever call you. I think 'selfless' suits you better."

Maia gave her mother another squeeze. "I take after you."

"Let's hope so!"

"I'm going to bring these clothes to Icarus, and then I'll be up. Good night."

"Good night."

Maia galloped down the stairs to the basement. She froze as her head poked out from under the ceiling. Icarus was standing completely naked in the middle of the basement.

"*Ahem*," said Maia. "Do you mind putting on a towel?"

"My apologies. I was about to get in the shower."

"Here," said Maia, tossing the t-shirt and boxer shorts. "I'll see you in the morning. Much *less* of you, I hope."

* * *

MAIA'S EYES OPENED WIDE. She looked at her alarm clock. It was 3:12am. Maia propped herself up on her elbows. Something *felt* wrong.

Schreeeeeeeech!

The noise came from below her bedroom window overlooking the backyard. Maia tiptoed over and looked out at the yard. It was empty.

Maia gazed up at the sky. Finding Polaris, she quickly connected several other stars to form constellations. Maia lingered on Orion for a moment. The constellation was named after the mighty hunter of ancient Greece. According to Greek mythology, Orion had so vigorously pursued Pleione, mother of the Pleiades, that Zeus turned her and her daughters into stars for their protection. Pleione had also been the wife of Atlas – before he renounced his godhood and eventually met and married Maia's mother. Maia traced her way across the heavens before settling on the Maia Nebula. She raised her hand to the sky to touch the star after which she'd been named.

Schreeeeeeeech!

The noise was far louder. A shadow fell across the backyard and disappeared just as quickly. Maia made her way down to the basement, taking care not to wake her parents and brother.

"Icarus, wake up!" Maia called. The futon was empty. "Icarus! Where are you?"

Schreeeeeeeech!

Maia turned to the basement window in time to see a sword scrape across the brick patio followed by a spiked tail. She grabbed a sword and shield and bounded up the stairs. Maia threw open the door to the backyard and flipped across the patio in a fighting stance. She was alone.

"What the hell?"

CLANG!

The sound of metal clashing metal came from the alley behind the garage. Maia ran to the source of the noise. Icarus stood between two of Circe's hybrid creatures. One had the upper body of a bear, talons for hands, and a tail that could've come from a dinosaur. The other had the head of an eagle and was wielding a sword. Maia slid in between Icarus and the eagle-headed creature and raised her own sword, cutting her opponent across the stomach. The creature let out a furious squawk as it swung its weapon. Maia leaned back as the sword passed in front of her eyes. Pulling herself forward, Maia plunged her sword into the creature's chest. A few feet away, Icarus had managed to slice off the bear-dinosaur hybrid's talons. The beast flayed the remainder of its arms, dosing Icarus with blood. Wiping his eyes, Icarus held up his shield and smacked the creature in its face. It stumbled backwards and Icarus lunged with his sword, slicing off the creature's head.

"Bloody hell!" cried Icarus, rubbing blood from his face. "Had I known he would be a gusher, I would have gone for the feet. Lord Zeus, what a mess!"

Despite the carnage before her, Maia smirked at Icarus's unexpected wit. She wasn't the only one who'd changed since their last adventure together. Maia kneeled next to the eagle-headed hybrid. Unlike Icarus's opponent, it had traces of clothing and armor. Maia removed its gauntlet and stepped into the driveway.

In the light of the moon, she was able to decipher a pattern in the metalwork.

"Icarus, this is an Amazon's gauntlet! That creature was—"

"An Amazon," said Icarus, bowing his head "Circe's reach has extended far across Olympia. The Amazons resist, but some have fallen."

A light appeared in a window, and a moment later Maia's father peered outside.

"Let's go. My parents are awake," said Maia.

"What about these... beasts?"

"It's still early. We'll have time to dispose of them before morning." Maia regretted her words almost immediately. One of the "beasts" was an Amazon, a sister she swore never to abandon. Despite the warrior's grotesque transformation, she deserved a funeral worthy of her rank.

Maia kneeled next to the fallen Amazon. "Though it was I who took your life, I will bring ruination to the one who caused it. I swear to you, my sister."

"Maia, there was no way for you to have known. Do not take this upon yourself."

"I have no intention of tormenting myself. I will find a coin to pay Charon to ferry my sister to the realm of the dead. And then I will allow my grief and anger to grant me the strength to make certain she is soon joined by Circe and her daughter."

CHAPTER SEVEN

SAYING GOODBYE

THE LAST OF A STACK of college brochures and flyers fluttered down from the top shelf of Maia's closet, leaving a cluttered pile at her feet. Maia kicked the papers to the side. Staring up at her was an advertisement for a local university showcasing a trio of college students of varying skin tone laughing as they ran across a field with a blurred clock tower in the background. "Make your mark!" insisted the logo across the bottom of the flyer. Maia stepped on and crumpled the jovial gang as she reached for a suitcase in the rear of the closet.

Maia tossed the suitcase onto her bed, knocking over the pile of clothing she'd been assembling for the last hour. She ran her hands through her hair as she considered some of her wardrobe choices. It was tough choosing what to wear on a trip to an otherworldly dimension that was likely to end in a war. Maia picked up a sweatshirt her parents had bought her in the fall on a visit to a university in New York City – one of their last efforts to get Maia to commit to a college. She ran her fingers over the logo, noticing for the first time a group of athletes, like those who participated in the games of ancient Greece, racing to grab a wreath of olive leaves. Maia dropped the sweatshirt into her suitcase. She'd learned long ago not to ignore signs.

Knock knock knock!

Icarus leaned his head into Maia's bedroom. "Pardon me, Maia, but I must take my leave. Triton is waiting."

"I'll come with you," said Maia. She scooped up a t-shirt and pair of shorts that'd fallen on the floor and laid them on her bed.

"You are busy," said Icarus. "There is no need to accompany me. I will see you in Varkiza."

Maia crossed the room and pulled the door open the rest of the way. Icarus was wearing a Peterson Construction tank top and cut-off camouflage shorts. "Looking sharp."

Icarus cocked his head. "Your mother assured me I could keep the shorts."

"I'm sure she did. She hates those. C'mon, let's go."

"Maia, please I insist—"

"It's fine. We don't have to leave for the airport for an hour. Besides, on my way back, I can stop at the drugstore in town and pick up some gum. It helps when I fly."

"Gum? Really? I always used wax," said Icarus, trying to contain a smile.

"Comedian," said Maia, shoving Icarus down the hallway. "Chewing gum helps your ears pop when you're on an airplane. No offense, but I'll take flying my way over yours."

"I've actually become quite expert since we last flew."

"No deep-sea plunges?"

"Fewer."

"Right. Mom! Dad! I'll be back in a little while," Maia called as they walked out the front door.

The afternoon was wearing on into evening, with a light sun shower. Maia sprang down her front steps with Icarus behind her. They crossed the lawn onto the sidewalk and walked in the direction of the beach. Maia and Icarus arrived at the corner of the block. Maia stopped, but Icarus stepped into the street into the path of an oncoming car.

"Whoa!" yelled Maia, yanking Icarus by his shirt back onto the sidewalk. The driver of the car honked his horn and gave Icarus the middle finger as he raced by.

"Oh, bite me," said Maia to the passing driver. "What the hell, Icarus? I know there aren't any cars in Olympia, but you have wagons and chariots, right?"

"Forgive me, Maia. My thoughts were... occupied."

Maia looked up and down the street before grabbing Icarus's hand and crossing onto the opposite side. They stepped to the left to allow a boy to pass on a bicycle with training wheels followed by a man pushing a baby carriage. Maia noticed a broad smile take over Icarus's face.

"Do you want children, Maia?"

"What? Oh, maybe someday. Why?"

"I would like children – many, many children."

"I'm sure you'll be a great father."

"I hope so," said Icarus, looking Maia in the eyes.

"What is it?"

"You are still holding my hand."

"*Oh!* Sorry," said Maia, pulling her hand away. "Um, let's go. You don't want to miss your ride."

Maia and Icarus walked in silence for several minutes. The rain began to fall in earnest, and they quickened their pace. As they came around a corner, Maia was relieved to see that the beach was empty.

They stepped onto the sand and trod over to a jetty of large boulders. Maia hopped onto a stone, followed by Icarus, and crab walked down the other side to a secluded section of the beach. Icarus flopped down next to her. Maia looked up to the cliffs that gave her hometown its name. A succession of cliff-side trees afforded them privacy from above.

"If you are worried about being seen, Maia, you do not have to stay. Triton will—"

"I'm not nervous," said Maia, taking a deep breath. "In fact, I'm pretty—"

FWOOOOOOSH!

A cone of water flew up into the sky. Several yards out in the harbor, the water boiled furiously. In the midst of the wild froth emerged the golden tines of a trident. It turned and a path to the surf spread open. Fish flopped back and forth amongst aluminum cans and plastic straws before re-submerging into the walls of seawater. At the opposite end of the path, balanced on a mighty tale of emerald green scales, Triton, son of Poseidon and reigning god of the sea, beckoned to Icarus.

"I have to go," said Icarus, taking Maia by the hand.

"How long will the journey take?"

"Three or four hours at most."

Maia thought back to her own harrowing undersea trip via Triton in Olympia, from a battlefield outside Athens to the garden of the Hesperides. It'd taken only a few minutes, but had more than satisfied any curiosity she held about the travel habits of merpeople.

"I'll see you in Varkiza," said Maia, hugging Icarus.

"I hope your flight is uneventful."

Maia chuckled. "That's funny coming from you."

Icarus shrugged and ran down the path forged by Triton. The walls of water crashed down, Icarus and Triton vanishing in their wake. The foam covering the water slowly dissipated.

Looking out at the settling water, Maia finished the statement she'd begun before Triton had appeared.

"I'm not nervous about being seen because I'm pretty sure I'm never coming back here."

* * *

MAIA BUCKLED HER BROTHER into his car seat. Jordi grabbed for Maia's ear, blowing a raspberry. Laughing, Maia wiped her face. "Thanks, little man, but I already took a shower."

Jordi continued to blow raspberries, prompting Maia to withdraw from the backseat of her father's black SUV.

"Here," she said, putting a stuffed panda bear in Jordi's lap. "Mr. Binks could use a rinse."

She peered up at her house, her attention drawn to one of the many alterations her father had made. The house had seemed so small when it was just Maia, her mother, and grandfather. Maia pictured Grandpa sitting on the front porch smoking a cigar. She waved at the imagined image.

"Saying goodbye to your house?" asked her best friend, Jackie, as she emerged from behind the SUV. "It's not like you to be sentimental."

Maia hugged her friend. "You made it! I was afraid I wasn't going to see you before we left."

"I can't believe you're going. Are you sure you're going to be safe?"

"My father says we'll be safer in Greece than in Sea Cliff. We're vulnerable here. At least in Greece, we'll be able to call on some friends for protection."

"'Friends'? You mean the Amazons? Yeah, I guess you'll be safer there. Where are your parents?"

"They just went back inside," answered Maia. "We're waiting for one of my dad's guys to come and drive us to the airport. What about you? Are you excited to go to Spain?"

"Yes!" cried Jackie. "But you'll be back before then, right? *Oh!* Or maybe if you're still in Greece, we could meet up. You could come to Spain, or I could go to Greece. Or we could meet up in some place like Italy. That'd be amazing!"

"That would be amazing," Maia said, breaking eye contact with Jackie.

"Maia, what is it?"

"It's nothing. In case I'm not back, I hope you have a great time with Roc. Remind him that lacrosse is a much better sport than soccer."

"Fútbol."

"Right. Fútbol."

"You *are* coming back?" asked Jackie.

A small pickup truck pulled in front of Maia's house, music blaring from the windows. Maia's parents walked out of the house. Matthias gestured at the driver of the pickup truck, and the music stopped.

"Hi, Jackie!" said Eleanor. "Maia, is Jordi buckled up?"

"Yes. Blowing raspberries in the comfort of air conditioning."

"It's nice of you to stop by," said Eleanor, hugging Jackie. "Maia, I think your dad wants to get going."

Maia nodded as her mother took a seat next to Jordi and closed the rear passenger door. She took Jackie by the hands and faked a smile.

"I'll be back."

"Maia, I've known you since kindergarten, and I can tell when you're lying," said Jackie, a tear rolling down her cheek. She ran her thumb over Maia's bracelet. "Just make sure you keep this on."

"I will."

"And I know you're an Amazon and everything, but if things get bad, you get out of there, okay?"

"I promise. Maybe I'll see you in Italy," offered Maia.

Jackie hugged Maia before turning away wordlessly. She waved at Maia's father as she crossed the street.

"Is Jackie alright?" asked Matthias.

"She's my best friend. She's worried."

"And you, Maia?"

"I gave that up five years ago," said Maia. "When the impossible *becomes* possible, worrying is just a waste of time."

CHAPTER EIGHT

FAMILY TIES

THE CAB RIDE FROM ATHENS INTERNATIONAL AIRPORT to Varkiza was punctuated by more than a few abrupt stops. Their driver cursed and swerved around trucks and other slower-moving vehicles, only to get stuck at several roadwork sites. Maia rolled down her window. Warm air flooded the cab, and Maia filled her lungs.

"Your father brings us to Greece for our safety, and this lunatic is going to get us killed before we even get unpacked," said Maia's mother. "I can't believe your uncle didn't show up at the airport. This isn't any safer than being at home."

"It's going to be okay, Mom," said Maia. "We're only a few exits away. Can you see the other cab?"

Eleanor stretched to look out the rear window of the cab. "I can't see crap, Maia."

"Whoa! Do you kiss Dad with that mouth?"

"Very funny. Okay, I'm sorry. No, I don't see their cab. I hope Jordi is okay. I don't know why I agreed to split up."

"We didn't have a choice. It's better this way. Dad can watch over Jordi, and I—"

"What?" interrupted Eleanor. "You get to watch over me?"

The cab screeched to a halt. The driver leaned into the car horn and screamed a string of obscenities. Maia grabbed the driver by the back of his neck and squeezed hard enough for him to gasp.

"Just drive," Maia said with gritted teeth.

Without another word, the driver maneuvered his way around the car in front of him and accelerated down the road.

"Maia, you could've hurt him," said Eleanor.

"Yeah, I could've," said Maia, rolling up her window. "Like I said, everything is going to be okay."

A few minutes later, the cab pulled up to a gate at the end of the long path that led to the front door of Maia's grandmother's house. The driver let Maia and her mother out before scrambling to the back of the car and emptying the trunk. Eleanor opened her purse, but the driver waved her off. He jumped back in the cab and raced off, one hand rubbing the back of his neck.

Maia put on her backpack. "Are you ready?"

"I think we should wait for your father," answered Eleanor, peering up at the house. "It looks the same."

"*Hmmm?*"

"The house. It looks the same as it did seventeen years ago."

"It looks the same as it did five years ago, too," said Maia. "I don't think Yaya cares much for change."

"It's funny to hear you call her that."

"I guess I could call her Hera, goddess of marriage and women. Seems a bit formal, but... "

Eleanor ignored her daughter. "The last time I was here, your grandmother was standing just where you are. She was crying and begging me to change my mind about leaving with you. I couldn't look at her. She pleaded with me to let her kiss you one more time, but I hurried into the cab and told the driver to go. You started crying, and I joined in – all the way to the airport." Eleanor bit her lip. "I never thought I'd be back here."

Maia wrapped her arms around her mother. "If you want to cry now, it's okay. I know how—"

"*Shhh!*"

"What's the matter?" whispered Maia.

"I think we're being watched. There's someone over... there!" yelled Eleanor.

Maia scoured the ground for an object to use as a weapon. Assuming a defensive position, she picked up a loose brick. "Stay behind me."

"Maia, please stop. It is only I, Icarus."

Maia threw down the brick. "Why were you hiding?"

"I was not hiding," said Icarus. "You were making so much noise, I came to investigate. I have been awaiting you. Where is your father?"

"He should be here any second. We had to take separate cabs."

"And your uncle?"

"Your guess is as good as mine."

The hum of a motor bounced off the walls lining the road. The cab carrying Matthias and Jordi emerged from around the corner and pulled up alongside Maia. Eleanor opened the door and freed Jordi from his car seat.

"There's my big guy. Oh, I missed you," said Maia's mother, snuggling Jordi in her arms.

Icarus helped Matthias unload the remaining luggage from the trunk while Maia uninstalled Jordi's car seat. Matthias tipped the driver. With a nod, the driver got back in his cab and pulled away.

"Maia, why'd you hurt your driver?" Matthias asked.

"Why would you ask that?"

"Because he radioed our driver as we were entering town and told him 'the girl with wild hair' nearly broke his neck."

Maia shrugged. "He wasn't driving safely, and it was making Mom nervous."

"*Ha!* Well, it was fortunate for him then he was paid upfront." Matthias approached his wife, still cradling Jordi. "No hug for me?"

"You! I'm about ready to strangle you! We're completely exposed out here. We've had a target on our backs from the second we stepped off the airplane!" yelled Eleanor.

"Look up."

"What?"

"I said—"

"I heard you. What's up there? All I see is... is that a winged horse?"

"There are two of them in fact, each ridden by one of Maia's Amazon sisters. They have been with us since the airport."

"Why can't we make them out more clearly, Dad?" asked Maia. "If you hadn't told me to look, I never would have noticed."

"Call it an Amazon trade secret, adéxios," said one of the riders from above. "*Heeya!*"

The winged steed, caramel in color except for its black mane and tail, swooped down, passing a few feet above Maia's head. Its rider jumped off and landed in front of Maia. The horse took back up to the sky.

"Captain Penelopeia!" cried Maia as she pulled the captain of the Amazon military in for a hug.

"It is good to see you, Maia," said Captain Penelopeia.

"The last time I saw you, you were in pretty bad shape," said Maia.

"The battle with Heracles and his forces was costly to many. I have long since recovered. But I have scars to remind me of my failure."

Maia motioned to introduce her mother, but she was distracted by a noise coming from the front door of the house. There stood her grandmother, known in a former life as Hera, wife of Zeus. Maia's lower lip trembled. Yaya had aged more than Maia had expected in five years. She stood unsteadily on the front steps supported on her right side by a gnarled wooden walking stick and on her left side by a young man in plain clothes with light eyes and a mop of sandy blonde hair. Maia and Yaya locked eyes, and the old woman smiled.

"Come," Yaya said softly, nodding her head. Tears filled her eyes. The man attending to Yaya put his arm around her and beckoned for her to enter the house. Yaya resisted, again whispering, "Come."

Maia threw open the gate and ran up the path, dropping to one knee in front of her grandmother. Tears ran down her face as she managed to squeak out, "Écho epistrépsei. I came back."

Yaya lifted her right arm and painstakingly extended her index finger. Trembling, she pointed at Maia's necklace.

"Yes, I still have it," said Maia, holding the coin at the end of the necklace her grandmother had given her five years prior. "I think of you every day."

Blinking back tears, Yaya pushed the young man away and put her arm out for Maia to take. "You eat?"

"I can't wait to see what you've made," said Maia as her grandmother steered her into the front entrance. Maia looked back at her parents and grinned.

* * *

A TEPID BREEZE GUSTED through the back patio of Maia's grandmother's house. Maia grabbed another shortbread cookie from the green translucent platter in front of her. In the chair next to her,

Jordi slept in their mother's arms. Maia's father and Icarus spoke quietly to each other in Greek, occasionally gesturing at Maia.

"Do either of you care to fill me in on your conversation? I only understand Greek when I'm in Olympia," said Maia, wiping powdered sugar from her upper lip with a napkin. "Plus Jordi can sleep through a freight train so there's no need to whisper."

"I'm tired of waiting for Dorian. Where is he? We have far too much to discuss for him to disappear," said Matthias.

"There is only one possible explanation. He is in Olympia and unable to return," said Icarus. "I will make the journey and find out what has happened to him."

"No one is going anywhere," said Eleanor. "We're safe, right? The Amazons are here to protect us. Don't make that face, Matt! It's been a long time, but I still remember enough Greek to know what you two were talking about. You're not taking on Circe by yourself. We're sticking to the plan. I'm sure Dorian will be here soon."

"Eleanor, do not—"

"Maia, please pass your father a cookie," said Eleanor. "Not another word about leaving."

Maia heaved herself upright in her chair. She reached for the peacock-shaped plate of shortbread cookies, but her father grabbed it before she could.

"I can help myself," Matthias said.

"Maybe I should go for a walk," said Maia. "Icarus, you should come, too. I think my parents need some private time."

One of the glass doors onto the patio opened, and Yaya's attendant stepped out. He squinted back and forth between Matthias and Eleanor.

"The boy takes after his mother, but you, Maia, you favor your father. You are not of this world."

"Excuse me? What do you know about—"

"Your grandmother is resting. Your arrival caused her too much excitement. Is there any baklava left?"

"I'm sorry, but I didn't catch your name," said Matthias.

"It is Apolyn. I introduced myself earlier, but you seemed preoccupied. Well, there is much going on, I suppose. Dorian will be here soon, by the way."

"And how do you know that?" asked Maia.

"I know things," said Apolyn, putting a forkful of baklava in his mouth.

"Apolyn is not a name you hear very often," said Matthias. "Where are you from?"

"*Ugh*, really? I will give you a hint. You need a chunk of Pandora's jar to get there."

"You are from Olympia! Dorian brought someone from Olympia to look after our mother."

"Not quite. I help with her because I live here... with Dorian," said Apolyn. "Can I have the cookies?"

"Enough with the cookies!" shouted Maia. She glanced over at Jordi. He stirred for a moment then let out a long gurgle and drifted back to sleep. "I'm very happy for you and Dorian, but we need him here."

"I told you—"

"Yes," interrupted Maia, "but how soon will he be here?"

A gate on the side of the house creaked open, and Captain Penelopeia, who'd been walking the property line, moved in the direction of the noise. A moment later, Dorian emerged from the side of the house. His lip was cut and his hair, usually meticulous, looked like it'd been under a mixer.

"Dorian, what kept you?" asked Matthias.

"Is that blood in your hair?" asked Maia.

Apolyn jumped up and hugged Dorian. "Is everything okay? Were you able to get to them?"

"Get to whom?" Maia asked.

"Our tribe – the Dorians."

"The ones you named yourself after."

"Obviously," hissed Apolyn.

"I am sorry, my love, but the Dorians are no more. The island of Crete is completely overrun by Circe's creatures. It is grimmer in Olympia than even I had imagined. If I had known, I would not have told you all to come."

"It's too late for regrets," said Matthias. "And there is but one recourse. I must go to Circe and put an end to this. It's the only way."

"Like hell it is, Matt," said Eleanor.

"I agree," said Dorian. "You would not be immune to her witchcraft and would suffer the same fate as the unfortunate creatures crawling over the whole of Olympia."

"What do you suggest, brother? We wait here for Circe? For all we know, she's plotting to cross the barrier to this world. No! I will not leave my family at risk."

"I do not believe that Circe has any interest in your family."

"How can you say that?" asked Maia. "We were attacked at our home in Sea Cliff. We only came here because you thought it'd be safer."

"It was not Circe who engineered that attack. It was her daughter Akantha. As I said, there is no reason to assume Circe herself has plans to cause you harm."

"Then I will reason with Circe," said Matthias. "She must control her daughter."

"Brother, you still consider Circe an ally because she helped us all those years ago. She cannot be trusted."

"Dammit, Dorian! Give me an occupation before I run mad!"

"*Waaaah!*"

Jordi was finally roused by the increasingly discordant words.

"It's okay," whispered Eleanor as she stood. "I'm going to take him inside. Matt, don't do anything rash."

Maia stood as well. "I'm going to go for a walk."

"I will join you," said Icarus.

"Maia, do not go too far," said her father. "Allow one of your sister Amazons to go with you."

"I will go," said Captain Penelopeia.

Maia crossed the patio and kissed her father on the forehead. "Listen to Mom. There's no reason we have to rush into anything."

"I pray you're correct," said Matthias.

"So do I," added Maia under her breath.

CHAPTER NINE

THE DEEPEST CUT

THE BEACH OVERFLOWED WITH SUNBATHERS. For a moment, Maia found herself envying the ease with which the residents of Varkiza and its many summer visitors lay on the sand or splashed in the cerulean waters. They were oblivious to the conflict occurring on the other side of an invisible barrier and its potential to cross over into their otherwise serene world. Maia passed a group of girls laughing fitfully as they walked off the sand onto a wooden boardwalk. They reminded her of her cousin Helena. She was still hospitalized in intensive care. *But why?* Maia asked herself. There was no logic behind the attacks. Akantha hated Maia for her perceived part in Akantha's father's downfall, but it seemed unlikely she could orchestrate the attacks on her own.

"Do you wish to walk on the sand?" asked Icarus.

"Yes, that'd be nice," answered Maia. "If we can find room. I can't believe how crowded this place is."

"I seem to recall that we had much more room to ourselves the last time we were here," said Icarus. "But I carry no weapons. I promise."

"Maybe you should be." Maia's eyes shifted from beachgoer to beachgoer, searching for anything out of the ordinary. She often thought of herself as a member of a security detail, like the Secret Service, but in this case she was protecting herself. Maia sat on the edge of the boardwalk and kicked off her flip-flops. The sand burned her toes. Icarus reached out his hand and pulled Maia to her feet. He was wearing a ring, Maia noticed for the first time. She turned his hand over. The ring was etched with wings.

"That's a beautiful ring," said Maia. "I'm surprised you'd go for a wings motif, all things considered."

Icarus laughed. "It was a gift. I would not have chosen the wings either. But it is... useful."

Maia raised an eyebrow, and Icarus turned away. They strolled in silence for a few minutes. Maia noticed Icarus looking at her sideways several times. There was clearly more to tell about the ring.

"So, maybe now is a good time for you to tell me how you're, you know, still alive. I mean, I get the whole 'actions have a way of repeating in Olympia' thing, but you took a pretty nasty plunge into the middle of the sea."

"I was fortunate enough to be rescued by a daughter of Triton."

"Pallas?"

"I am impressed by your knowledge of what you call 'myth.' No, it was not Pallas. Sadly, she remains in the Underworld, yet another victim of Lord Zeus's cruelty. Pallas's sister Kalliste saved me. It was she who gave me the ring."

"Wow, she rescued you *and* gave you a ring. Did you give her anything?"

"I gave her my hand in marriage," said Icarus.

"Oh."

Two boys, no older than seven, came barreling between Maia and Icarus, kicking sand into their faces. Maia blinked away the intrusive particles, but didn't break eye contact with Icarus. He was married.

"Maia, perhaps I should have said something sooner."

"Like when you showed up in Sea Cliff?"

Icarus looked at his feet. "You are angry."

"No, I mean, yes. *Ugh!* No, I'm not angry that you're married, but I don't understand why you kept it a secret."

"When I was first tasked with journeying to Sea Cliff, I felt a tremendous amount of guilt. I was aware of your time in Olympia two years ago when you battled Heracles, but I did not go to offer you assistance. I remained by my wife's side, though I owed you."

"You don't owe me anything, Icarus, not even an explanation about—"

"Yes, I do!" yelled Icarus. A group of teenagers a few feet away turned and stared. Icarus's face went red. Two girls pointed and snickered.

"Oh, c'mon," said Maia, pulling Icarus toward the water. She waded in ankle deep and beckoned Icarus to join her.

Icarus's shoulders dropped. Shaking his head, he stepped into the water. "Forgive me."

"What is it you think you owe me?"

Icarus looked back at the beach, searching for something amongst the beachgoers. Finally, he pointed and nodded at Maia to look. "It was there that I fired the arrow that... ruined your life." His arm fell to his side. The corners of Icarus's mouth drooped, revealing years of regret.

"I was a fool. I brought you to Olympia and to the attention of those that now seek you harm. You would be safe if not for my reckless actions. I should never have done that, but, more importantly, when your life was in danger from Heracles, I should have been by your side. I owed you that and much more than I can ever repay."

Maia waited to see if Icarus had more to say, but it seemed clear that he'd said beyond what even he'd intended. As his eyes drifted to the sea, Maia took his hand and squeezed it.

"Bullshit."

Icarus's head snapped back, and he squinted at Maia. "I beg your pardon."

"That's ridiculous. Do you think for a moment that I regret finding out the truth behind my father's disappearance? Do you think I would change one damn thing about the last five years? My parents are back together. I have a brother. And I refuse to believe for a second that I wouldn't have ended up in Olympia without your intervention. We've already been through this. You just played a part in a storyline fate had already written. My father agrees."

"But you're in danger."

"I would've been anyway. And maybe I'd be in even more danger if things had played out differently," said Maia. "I wouldn't change a thing. I'm an Amazon, for Hera's sake."

Icarus furrowed his brow and shook his head, but ultimately a broad grin took over his face. It reminded Maia of how he looked when they first met.

"My wife was right to be jealous," said Icarus. "You are incredible."

"Your wife is jealous of me? Don't get me wrong, you gave me a few butterflies when you helped me escape from King Alphaios's castle, but I'm much happier to call you a friend."

Icarus pulled Maia into his arms. "As am I."

"*AAAAIIIIIIEEEEE!*"

A few feet away, a young girl was screaming. Maia followed the girl's gaze. Several feet out in the water emerged the head of a shark. Instinctively, Maia reached for a sword, but came up empty handed. The shark continued to rise, revealing the body of a man. It was another of Circe's hybrids! All around her, people began to scream as another hybrid with the tentacles of an octopus broke the surface of the water, followed by another that looked like a cross between an alligator and a python.

"We have to get everyone out of here," cried Icarus. He yelled at the beachgoers in Greek as he ran up the beach.

"Alala!" called Captain Penelopeia from above. She dismounted her winged steed and landed by Maia's side with a burlap sack. "Here," Captain Penelopeia said, holding out a sword and shield she'd retrieved from the sack.

Maia turned just as the shark hybrid leapt out of the water. Maia knocked him aside with her shield, spun and sliced off the creature's dorsal fin. Captain Penelopeia plunged her sword into the beast's head.

Icarus ran toward them. "I need a weapon!"

Captain Penelopeia kicked the sack at Icarus. He dropped to his knees and pulled out a bow and quiver of arrows. Icarus loaded an arrow and fired it, striking the octopus hybrid in the chest.

"Let us hope his heart is still where it belongs." Icarus let fly another arrow, and it struck the alligator hybrid in the eye. It fell backward under the water.

"We need to get to higher ground," said Captain Penelopeia.

A volley of screams came from the direction of the boardwalk. The fleeing beachgoers were blocked by a swarm of hybrids.

"We have to help them," said Maia.

"And we will, sister," said Captain Penelopeia, leading the charge up the beach.

Maia ran toward a young mother and her baby, hurling her sword at a creature threatening to attack them. She struck the hybrid in the chest. As Maia skidded in front of the mother and her baby, she lifted her shield over her head and brought it down on the creature's head, rendering it lifeless. Maia grabbed her sword and ran toward the crowd.

"Follow me!" she cried, waving her sword and hoping that the people understood her desire to lead them to safety. Maia sliced the legs off a beast part woman, part wolf and knocked another to the ground with her shield. A raptor-looking hybrid jumped from behind a tent, and Maia dropped back, trying to give herself enough room to swing her sword. A familiar twang sounded behind her, and an arrow stuck out from the creature's throat. Maia watched Icarus. He was firing arrows and retrieving them just as quickly. Maia scrambled to her feet, clearing a path for the remaining beachgoers. Sirens sounded in the distance, followed by gunfire.

Hearing Icarus cry out in pain, Maia ran back to the sand. She nearly dropped her sword at the sight of Aeton, a vile sadistic servant of Akantha's father, King Alphaios, she'd encountered five years before. He stood over Icarus with a sword. Maia threw her shield, but Aeton ducked. He raised the sword, and shrieked in pain as Icarus stabbed him in the thigh with an arrow. Maia ran forward and smacked the sword from Aeton's hands.

Maia stood over Aeton, her sword pointed at his throat. Icarus pulled himself up next to her.

"Are you okay?" Maia asked.

"He only hit me with the hilt."

Aeton laughed. "I like to play with my food before I eat it."

Maia pushed the sword forward, nicking Aeton's chin.

"I thank you for allowing us to keep you occupied," spat Aeton. "My mistress will have the one she seeks."

"What are you talking about?" cried Maia.

"You are too late," said Aeton.

"Maia, his hand!" called Icarus.

Aeton tightened his fist, and an explosion of light signaled that he'd escaped to Olympia.

"We have to get home," Maia said, scouring the beach.

Captain Penelopeia ran back toward Maia and Icarus. "All of Circe's beasts have been vanquished. But the area is crawling with... your people's soldiers."

"Police officers. How are we going to explain these weapons?"

"Leave them. Go back to your grandmother's house. I will be right behind you." Captain Penelopeia whistled, and her horse dove from above. "Go!"

Maia and Icarus ran up the beach, past the boardwalk toward the dunes. They leapt over a dune fence and climbed over a hill of sand and beach grass. Maia jumped down, and Icarus followed. They squeezed behind a wall of stones and emerged in someone's backyard. They made their way to the front and ran up the road toward Maia's grandmother's house.

"Maia!" cried her father from the other side of the road. Dorian was by his side. "Are you alright?"

Maia ran across the street and into her father's arms. "I'm fine. Are you okay?"

"Yes. We heard the screams and came running."

"We were attacked by Circe's hybrids. And that psychotic piece of crap who worked for Akantha's father, Aeton! He said you were in danger! I thought they'd gotten you."

"Aeton said I was in danger?"

"He said he was just trying to keep me busy so his 'mistress' could get the one she wants."

"We must get home," said Matthias.

They ran back in silence. Matthias burst through the gate, up the path and into the house. Maia caught up to him as his voice filled the dwelling.

"Eleanor! Eleanor, where are you?"

They moved into the main living area of the house. Maia gasped as she recognized a pair of boots from behind a table. One of her Amazon sisters lay on the floor, blood pooled by her head.

Muffled moans came from the kitchen. Maia pushed the door open. Her grandmother was on the floor crying, supported by Apolyn. "Is she okay?"

"She is not hurt," answered Apolyn.

Dorian pushed his way past Maia and dropped to the floor.

Maia ran back into the living room. Her father came out of a bedroom.

"I can't find—"

"Matt!" cried Eleanor as she stumbled out of a closet. She was bleeding from the head. Matthias clutched her as she fell.

"They took him! They took the baby. I tried to fight them, but there were too many." Eleanor wailed in pain, and her husband pulled her into his arms. "They took Jordi!"

Matthias turned to Maia, tears staining his face. He stroked his wife's hair. Her sobs echoed through the house.

Captain Penelopeia arrived, followed by Icarus. Dorian entered from the kitchen. Matthias glared at the trio.

"Go."

Icarus nodded at Maia's uncle. Dorian pulled a piece of Pandora's jar from his pocket and grabbed Icarus by the wrist. There was a burst of light, and they vanished. Captain Penelopeia put her hand on Maia's shoulder before exiting. A moment later there was another flash of light from the front of the house.

"I'm going, too," said Maia.

"You're not going anywhere," said her father as he rocked her mother in his arms. Matthias closed his eyes. His hands trembled.

Maia struggled to breathe. Her mother's pain radiated like a raging wildfire. Maia spied a bloody handprint on the doorframe of her grandmother's guest room. As she passed through the doorway, she bent down to pick up a sword left by her fallen sister. Maia dragged the sword as she surveyed the damage. The bed was overturned, and a dresser was on its side. The framed pictures that'd covered the dresser were scattered on the floor surrounded by shards of glass. Poking out from under the bed was Mr. Binks, Jordi's favorite stuffed animal. Maia picked up the stuffed panda bear and pressed it to her forehead.

"Hang on, little man – *sniff!* – just hang on. I'm coming for you."

INTERLUDE I

WHEN ELEANOR MET MATTHIAS

I CAN'T BELIEVE THIS. The hostel is supposed to be *right* here. And you know what, forget Angela. She totally ditched me. I guess she found something – or someone – at the train station more important to occupy her time.

It's over 100 degrees in Athens, and I'm hoping the ferociously foul smell filling my nostrils is from the dumpster at the curb and not me. I haven't showered in three days. Whoever said backpacking around Europe was the height of romance was full of it. Actually, I don't think anyone has ever said that.

I decide to walk around the block again. Maybe I've got the address of the hostel wrong. I find myself in a sea of outdoors chairs and tables, and my stomach does a series of summersaults. For the moment, I ignore my highly offensive body odor and savor the smell of the lamb, steak, and roasted vegetables being brought to the tables. It's been even longer than my last shower that I've had a decent meal. Or at least a meal that didn't consist of chocolate bars and soda. I pause a little too long next to a table covered in baklava and custard pies, and I get the stink-eye from a waiter. It's nice to know that some expressions cross international borders.

As I approach the corner of the block, a group of tourists led by a woman holding a purple binder in one hand and a tall plastic sunflower in the other march past me. I stare at their clothing, trying to figure out where they're from. Over the last few weeks,

I've gotten quite good at guessing someone's place of origin before I hear him or her speak. This particular group is from Spain, something tells me. This is confirmed when I hear a pair of girls be scolded by their mother for lagging behind. I look at them sympathetically, and one girl sticks her tongue out at me. Whatever. I'm glad her mother gave her crap.

A minute later, another tour group passes. I chew on my lips. I'm hungry and tired, and I've lost all patience. I push my way through the crowd and turn the corner. And I'm awed by what I've stumbled across. It's the entrance to the Acropolis. I was hoping to visit there after checking into the hostel, but I'm tempted to go now. I'm still staring when I feel a tap on my shoulder.

I turn and am awed again. The owner of the hand that touched my shoulder is smiling at me, and for a moment I am drowning in someone's ocean-grey eyes. He's gorgeous.

"Are you need help?" he asks.

My backpack nearly slips off onto the sidewalk. He's a few inches taller than me and capped off by a mop of curly brown hair that'd I'd love to run my fingers through.

"Um, yeah, I guess. I'm looking for a youth hostel that's supposed to be on this block," I answer. "Do you know where... "

I stop talking because he's staring at me. And I'm staring at him. And I could give a damn if I ever make it to the hostel. Or see the Acropolis for that matter.

"Um, hi." I talk good.

"Hello."

"So, about that hostel... "

"I take you for place to stay. Better than hostel," he says. "I am Matthias."

"I'm Eleanor," I manage to squeak out. Am I really thinking of letting a complete stranger take me someplace? This is the kind of hunger-induced stupidity my mother warned me about. But somehow I find myself nodding. Matthias takes my backpack and motions for me to follow him.

"Where are we going?"

"Sounion," Matthias answers.

"No, no, no," I say. "I'm staying in Athens."

"You like Sounion. You see."

I've never been to Sounion, but I know from my *Let's Go Europe* book that it's not in Athens proper. I reach out to take my backpack, and, while Matthias doesn't resist, he makes the saddest face I've ever seen.

"Let me take you, please. If not like, I bring back to Athens. I make promise."

Matthias reaches out to take my backpack, flashing a smile that gives me pause. But it also sends sparks through me. I let go of the backpack, and Matthias throws it over his shoulder. He reaches out his hand, and I take it. More sparks. As we walk hand in hand down the street, I have the oddest thought.

My mother is never going to let me out of her sight again.

CHAPTER TEN

AMONGST SISTERS

QUEEN HIPPOLYTA SAT UPON HER MIGHTY STEED, Lampus, a gift from the fallen goddess Eos. As brightly as Lampus shined, the queen's armor lacked luster in comparison. Queen Hippolyta, though never failing to maintain a royal bearing, carried a weariness that marked her face like a child with chickenpox. The daily battles with Circe's beasts had taken a toll on the Amazons, and Queen Hippolyta silently counted those lives lost. Just yesterday, another Amazon had made the journey to the Underworld. Even at the height of the conflict with Heracles, when Queen Hippolyta herself had been gravely wounded, there was no question that the Amazons would prevail. This war felt different, and Queen Hippolyta reluctantly admitted that she was at a loss for a next step. Behind her stood two Amazons, each bearing a shield and a spear. Like their queen, her guards wore battered armor and haunted expressions beneath their helmets.

Several yards ahead of Queen Hippolyta appeared a spot devoid of color. The space surrounding the spot twisted and pulled back as if yanked by a corkscrew. A moment later, the spot expanded out, and there was a flash of light. In its place stood Maia and her parents. The queen managed a weak smile. She dismounted Lampus and walked toward the Peterson family.

"Welcome back to Olympia," said Queen Hippolyta, her forceful voice betraying none of her doubt.

"Allow me to introduce my wife. This is Eleanor," said Matthias. He put his arm around Maia's mother, and she immediately began to cry. Matthias pulled her into a hug. "My love, this is Queen Hippolyta. She's going to help us find Jordi."

Eleanor let out a wail of such intensity that Queen Hippolyta's bottom lip quivered. Maia leaned into her parents, a single tear rolling down her cheek to her chin. She wiped it with her hand, and in doing so looked down at her outfit. She'd almost forgotten that her clothing changed when she crossed the barrier to Olympia. Maia wore a cobalt blue tunic and sandals. Her parents were similarly dressed in matching red tunics.

Queen Hippolyta turned to her guards. "Please escort Lord Matthias and Lady Eleanor to my quarters."

Matthias nodded and coaxed his wife to follow the guards with him. Eleanor sobbed as she allowed herself to be brought along by her husband. One of the guards pulled back an invisible curtain, and Maia's parents disappeared behind it.

"Thank you, Queen Hippolyta," said Maia, bowing. "We're eternally grateful for your hospitality." She raised her head and locked eyes with the queen.

"You are an Amazon, Maia. It is not hospitality you are offered, but your rightful place."

"I'm sorry about Kore," said Maia.

"As am I. But I am equally sorry that she was unable to prevent the attack on your family," said Queen Hippolyta. "Your mother suffers deeply, as do you and your father." The queen thrust her staff into the ground, kicking up a cloud of dust. "It is madness. There is no reason behind Circe's actions."

"Akantha hates me."

"If only this were about that traitorous hag," said Queen Hippolyta, eliciting a small smile from Maia. "No, there is something much more nefarious at play. While Heracles sought to conquer Olympia and bring his forces to the homeworld, Circe and her daughter seek only destruction. Entire settlements have been leveled, overrun by Circe's foul, twisted beasts. The population of Olympia has dwindled down to nothing."

"And the Amazons?" asked Maia.

"Our tribe endures, but we have suffered a great many losses. Some of our sisters have even been transformed by Circe's magic into the very creatures we have been battling."

"I know," said Maia, her chin shaking. "I'm so sorry, but I killed one of our—"

"Stop!" interrupted Queen Hippolyta. "Captain Penelopeia has told me what happened at your home. You bear no responsibility for that. Our sister died the moment Circe cast her spell. Your act was one of mercy."

Maia chewed the inside of her cheek. Tears ran down her face as she stepped toward Queen Hippolyta. "I've missed you."

"And I have missed you as well," said Queen Hippolyta, spreading her arms.

Maia fell into Queen Hippolyta's embrace and closed her eyes. They stood, supporting each other for several seconds, both seemingly relieved by the other's presence.

"*KEEEEEEARRR!*"

Overhead, a pair of winged horses jockeyed by Amazons patrolled the area shielded by Gaia's protective shroud. For all the pain and strife she'd witnessed in Olympia, the sight of a winged horse still made Maia's stomach flutter.

"Did you ever return to Pontus?" Maia asked, stepping back.

"We did, but it was for naught. Heracles reduced our city to rubble, far beyond salvation. We have maintained a nomadic existence since we last saw each other. In truth, it is better this way.

Though we do not have the security of a city wall, we are able to change our location more readily."

"A moving target is harder to hit."

"*Ha!* That is one point of view," said Queen Hippolyta.

"What do we do now?"

Queen Hippolyta unsheathed a sword from its casing on her back and held it out to Maia. "We bring your brother home. And we ensure that no other must endure your parents' pain."

Maia grasped the grip of the sword, examining the decorative engravings on the blade. It was the sword gifted to her two years before, when she recited the oath that officially brought her into the Amazon sisterhood. It was heavier than the swords with which she'd been practicing, and it seemed to hum as she cut an arc in the air. Wondrous, Maia thought, and for the moment she was certain that she'd see Jordi again.

* * *

MAIA PULLED BACK THE FLAP of the tent serving as the Amazon's armory and stepped into their camp. If holding her sword had given her a charge, being suited in full armor, crafted by her sister Amazons, caused lightning to course through her veins. Though pained to not know where Jordi was held, Maia moved through the camp with conviction. She wanted to hear everything the Amazons had been able to uncover about Circe's location.

Maia marveled at the flurry of activity kept hidden behind Gaia's invisible shroud. While smaller in number than when she last walked amongst the Amazons, there was no less intensity or purpose evident in each of her sister's actions. Swords clanged. Arrows sailed. Shields blocked. Whatever losses they'd mourned hadn't deterred the Amazons from forging a path back to the battlefield.

"If anyone seeks to bring ruin to our ways I will oppose this, so far as I am able by myself and with the help of my sisters," Maia recited as she made her way to Queen Hippolyta's tent. No other part of the Amazon oath resonated as much with Maia. The ways of the Amazons were just. They were not merely warriors. The Amazons were as bound by love as they were by combat. To seek to bring ruin to the Amazons was to seek to extinguish hope itself.

"Maia!" called her father as he exited a tent to the right of her. "There you are. I didn't know you'd gone to the armory."

"Where were you? Why aren't you with Mom?"

"Do not fret, Maia. I didn't leave your mother alone. She's with Queen Hippolyta. I went looking for herbs to help your mother sleep."

"You could use some sleep, too," said Maia.

"I will sleep when I have your brother in my arms."

Maia studied her father's eyes. Normally, they held a spark. His ocean-gray eyes danced even in the darkest times. But the spark was missing, and his eyes had lost all sense of rhythm. Maia grabbed her father's hand.

"Let's go see Mom," Maia said, pulling at her father.

Moments later, they entered Queen Hippolyta's tent. The sight before them wasn't what Maia had expected to see. Eleanor and the queen were laughing. Maia hadn't thought it possible for her mother to exhibit any other emotion than despair at this time. But she was laughing, and Queen Hippolyta was equally amused.

"Oh, come in, come in," said the queen. "Your mother was just recounting how challenging it was to... what did you call it?"

"Potty train," answered Eleanor.

"Potty train," repeated Queen Hippolyta. "What are 'M&M's'? They sound delightful."

"I'm sorry, but did I step into the wrong tent? Maybe the wrong hidden world? What the hell is going on here?"

Eleanor let out a breath strong enough to extinguish a torch. "Oh, that felt good. I've been holding onto that for days. Maia, you didn't do Queen Hippolyta justice. She's funnier than Emma Thompson."

Matthias moved to his wife's side. "Eleanor, I am so pleased to see you—"

"Not crying?"

"Well, yes, as a matter of fact."

"I'm taking a break from that. Queen's orders," Eleanor added before getting to her feet. "Matt, why don't you show me around the camp. Thank you, Queen Hippolyta."

"There is no need to thank me, Lady Eleanor. Anyone capable of raising a warrior such as Maia is beyond reproach and worthy of every form of respect I can offer."

Matthias and Eleanor exited the tent, their fingers intertwined. Maia watched in joyful disbelief.

"What did you say to her?" asked Maia.

"It is not what I said to her. It is what she said to me. Your mother is a remarkable woman. I merely encouraged her to use her pain and fear to strengthen her resolve; to drive her, not drown her. It is the way of the Amazons."

"Are you going to induct her, too?" asked Maia, her eyes narrowed.

"Perhaps in time," answered Queen Hippolyta. "But for the time being, I am content in getting to know her better. I was not exaggerating about the esteem in which I hold her."

"Because of me?"

"Yes, because of you, child of two worlds. A lesser individual would have given way long ago."

The corners of Maia's mouth dropped. "My mom is pretty badass. I should tell her that more often."

"We rarely do."

"What?"

"Honor those who reared us, of course," said Queen Hippolyta.

"Forgive me, your highness, but did you have parents?"

"Maia, what manner of question is that? Do you think I was carved from clay and given life by the gods?"

"Um, no, but I just—"

"Once we have rescued your brother and thwarted Circe and her fool of a daughter, you will spend some time in the Amazon archives."

"Please tell me you're joking," said Maia.

"I never joke when it comes to knowledge," said Queen Hippolyta as she approached the opening to the tent. "I must speak to Captain Penelopeia. I suggest you stay here and find something to read."

Maia shook her head as Queen Hippolyta exited the tent.

"So, yeah, that took an awkward turn."

CHAPTER ELEVEN

THE SON OF JASON

MAIA'S NOSE CRINKLED at the stink of piles of manure. The Amazons hadn't been keeping their stables as clean as to which she'd been accustomed. They had bigger fish to fry, Maia thought. She trailed her hand across the makeshift barricade, scanning the area for Xenophon, the horse that'd carried her into battle against Heracles's forces. She doubted she'd find him. Maia could only imagine what could've happened to the steed in the two years she'd been away.

"Admiring the herd?" asked Maia's father.

"There's not much to admire," answered Maia without turning around. "How's Mom?"

"She's asleep."

"What'd you give her?"

"Nothing, Maia. Your mother was exhausted."

Matthias's cheeks were stubbly and blotchy. There were dark circles under his eyes.

"You don't look so great, Dad. You should probably join Mom for a while."

Matthias looked past Maia. He rubbed his chin and let out a profound sigh. "It took me a long time to get used to sleeping. When I first gave up immortality, I hadn't expected that I'd get so tired. On my first night as a mortal, I collapsed into a fire pit. To my good fortune, the fire was largely extinguished. But I learned two lessons. I was required to sleep. And I could be injured. It was humbling. Still, I never enjoyed sleeping until I met your mother. Sleeping beside her, our bodies entwined—"

"Too much information."

"*Ahem.* Our bodies entwined, I finally understood what others spoke about when they extolled the virtues of sleep."

"That's really sweet, Dad."

"I hope you are as fortunate as I am to find a great love."

"And now we've gotten into questionable territory again."

"*Ha!* You are too easy, little star."

Maia blushed at her father's nickname for her. "Was there anything else you missed about being a Titan?"

"Missed? No. It was a burden, literally and figuratively. Bearing the cosmos on my shoulders was no more troubling than watching the ease with which my fellow Titans and the gods of Olympus trifled with humanity. Had I not been anchored in place, perhaps I too would've been so cruel."

"I doubt that very much, Dad."

"Power corrupts," said Matthias. "Look around. Olympia is the ultimate example of corruption. I'm more certain than ever that Zeus was wrong to create Olympia. The gods were meant to perish at the end of the Trojan War."

"How can you say... " Maia trailed off, distracted by the sound of horses – many horses – approaching the stables. Clouds of dust enveloped the stables, and Maia covered her mouth to keep from choking.

A horse skidded to a halt in front of her, its rider obscured by the soil kicked up. "*Whoa! Whoa!*" called the rider in a deep male voice. "Well, well, well." The rider slid off his steed and removed his helmet. "Hey, firecracker. Long time no see."

Maia stared at the young man standing in front of her. It was Nate, he of the blue-grey eyes and questionable taste in ball teams.

Nate, who'd protested he knew nothing of the existence of Olympia. Maia stepped forward, and Nate smiled. Maia pulled her arm back and flung her fist into Nate's cheek, his grin replaced by a staggered expression. Nate fell to the floor, knocking into his horse. The steed reared back, and Matthias ran forward to calm the animal.

"Maia! What's wrong with you?" cried her father as he fought to hold onto the horse's reins.

"Damn, firecracker," said Nate, rubbing his cheek. "Where'd you learn to punch like that?"

"Here, you jackass, in Olympia. You know, the place you swore you knew nothing about!"

"Maia, please calm down," said her father.

"No, no, it's alright, um, Mr. Peterson. I deserved that," said Nate, pulling himself to his feet.

"Call me Matthias."

"Dad, don't be nice to him. What the hell are you doing here, Nate? And where've you been?"

"I've been here in Olympia, Maia. I came back after my father died to assume my responsibilities. Look, I know I owe you an apology."

"Screw the apology. I'll take an explanation."

"And you'll have that, too. Maybe there's somewhere we can go and talk... in private," said Nate.

Maia took her eyes off Nate long enough to finally notice they were surrounded by several men on horseback. "They're with you?"

"Yes," answered Nate with a crooked grin.

"Captain?" began one of the men.

"It's alright, Tydeus. Take care of the horses. I have to go make things right with Maia."

* * *

MAIA KEPT HER EYES FORWARD. She was tempted to rub her fist, but she didn't want to give Nate any indication that the punch had hurt her hand. Her breathing was shallow. Despite the anger that flooded her face, Maia had to admit there was also a twisting sensation in her stomach. Nate looked good in armor. Maia tried to push the thought out of her head, but it continued to evade her like a fly at a picnic.

"Where are we going, firecracker?" asked Nate.

"Don't call me that."

"I'm sorry."

"And don't apologize. It makes you look weak."

"Maia, I was just knocked on my ass by a girl in front of my men. You don't think I already look weak?"

Maia spun and grabbed Nate by his wrist. "I'm not a 'girl'. I'm an Amazon. And you're in our camp, so speak with respect."

Nate frowned. "It was just a joke."

"There's nothing funny about this!" shouted Maia. "Do you even know why I'm back in Olympia?"

"I know about your brother. That's why I'm here."

Maia looked over Nate's shoulder. "Go inside," said Maia, pointing to a nearby tent. She pulled open the flap, and her nostrils were flooded with the scent of spices and cured meats. Her stomach rumbled. "This will have to do."

Nate followed her into the tent. Maia grabbed a crate and tossed it at Nate.

"Aren't you going to sit, Maia?"

"I'm not sure how long I'm staying. Start talking."

Nate sat on the crate. He ran his hand across his cheek and winced. "Queen Hippolyta would be proud."

Maia raised her eyebrows until they nearly touched her hairline.

"I'm like you," said Nate.

"What does that mean?"

"I'm a child of two worlds. My father was also from Olympia. You may've heard of him. His name was Jason."

"As in 'and the golden fleece'?"

"The one and the same. My dad was the leader of the Argonauts."

Maia thought back to Sea Cliff. "Icarus said the Argonauts had joined with the Amazons. He said Jason's son was leading them. That's... you."

"So, Icarus finally decided to show himself to you? Did you punch him, too?"

"No, actually, I gave him a hug. I was happy to see *him*."

"Look, Maia, I really do apologize for—"

"I told you I don't want an apology! Why does everyone feel the need to keep saying they're sorry?" Maia locked eyes with Nate. "If you'd been honest with me two years ago, you wouldn't need to apologize."

"Fine!" said Nate, standing up. "No more apologies. But you better get something straight. This place doesn't revolve around you. I had my reasons for keeping quiet."

"But you didn't have to lie. We'd been writing back and forth to each other for nearly two years, until you dropped off the face of the earth three months ago and my letters all came back unread. You never once thought to tell me about your father? And now he's dead, and... I feel like such an idiot."

"I never lied to you, Maia. And you made it pretty clear from the get go that certain topics were off limits."

"Because you pretended you didn't know about Olympia, even after you made that stupid comment when you kissed me. You were there when my parents were reunited. That was your opportunity to... "

"To what?"

Maia shifted her eyes downward. "To let me know I wasn't alone."

Nate's shoulders dropped. He inched forward, looking for a reaction. Encouraged by the lack of flying fists, Nate took two steps and grabbed Maia in his arms. She stiffened, her nose buried in Nate's shoulder. He smelled like almonds.

"I wanted to tell you, but it wasn't my decision to make."

Maia pulled herself free from Nate's embrace. "What did you mean about this place not revolving around me?"

Nate cocked his head. "Did you think it does?"

"No, I mean, of course not, but I only know what I've experienced. King Alphaios was obsessed with capturing me. Heracles wanted me so he could get to my father." Maia's cheeks went red. "I guess I didn't give much thought to whatever else was going on in Olympia."

"Well, I can't say I blame you. It's hardly worth the effort, especially now." Nate paced back and forth. "Honestly, Maia, I hate this place. When I found out about my dad, you'd think I'd be excited, right? But I realized pretty quickly the truth about Olympia."

"And what's that?"

"It's completely bogus. Zeus created Olympia to keep himself from blinking out of existence. The people here, including the Amazons and the Argonauts, were nothing more than playthings.

And now, to add insult to injury, they're all dying, hunted down by a crazy witch and her grotesque pets."

"Then why are you here?"

Nate rubbed his chin. He stared straight at Maia, a smile curling on his face. "I guess a good captain goes down with the ship."

"Nate... "

"Because I promised my father. He never intended to leave here. His first wife, Medea, was a pretty crazy witch herself. She punished him for getting engaged to another woman by sending him to our world, not long after your father first made the trip. Five years ago, he was finally able to make his way back."

"That's when I first came to Olympia."

"Yeah, I reckon he must've sensed the barrier being breached, and he found a way to do it himself. I don't doubt that he loved my mother, my sister, and me, but Olympia was his true home. Its people mattered to him. And if the Amazons and Argonauts are going to try to stop Circe from destroying it all, I'm going to stand with them." Nate unsheathed a sword hanging from his belt. "But now there's an even more important reason to fight. I'm going to help you find your brother."

Maia grabbed Nate by the sides of his head and pulled him in for a kiss. When she stepped back, she was smiling.

Nate dropped the sword. "What was that for?"

"Consider it my apology for punching you."

"Dang, firecracker. You can use me as a punching bag if that's how we're going to end each sparring session."

The twisting sensation in Maia's stomach returned.

"No promises."

CHAPTER TWELVE

A LACK OF CONFIDENCE

MAIA PUSHED THROUGH THE TENT FLAP and walked smack into her father.

"Where'd you go?" asked Matthias. "I've been looking for you all over camp."

Nate stuck his head out. "Uh, hi Mr. Peterson, um, Matthias. Uh, how are you?"

Matthias's eyes narrowed to slits, and Maia heard Nate swallow like he had ten pieces of gum in his mouth. "Nate and I were just talking. We had some catching up to do."

"I'm sure you did," said Matthias, his eyes continuing to bore a hole in Nate's forehead. "Your men are awaiting your return. That is, I should say your men *and* woman."

"Woman? Don't tell me you're married, too?"

Nate blushed, and Maia couldn't help but smirk. She enjoyed seeing him squirm.

"No, I'm not married. The Argonauts are an equal opportunity band of heroes... and heroines. C'mon, I'll introduce you."

"I'm sure Queen Hippolyta is eager to hear about your reconnaissance mission."

"I wish I had more to report, Matthias. Her beasts roam every inch of Olympia, but Circe is nowhere to be found."

Nate's words stabbed at Maia's side. Circe had her brother. And she couldn't bear the thought of another day passing without Jordi safely with her parents.

"Very well. Dorian and Icarus have yet to report back. Perhaps they've had some success. I'll be with your mother if you need me."

Maia felt a weight pressing on her as she watched her father walk away. This man that stood for a millennia with the cosmos on his back looked like he could be knocked over by a satyr.

A woman of considerable size suddenly blocked Maia's path. Instinctively, she reached for her sword.

"Captain Nathaniel, the men are hungry."

"For real? This isn't their first time in this camp. They know where to get food. These guys can cross the sea, dodging sirens and giant, rock-throwing bronze automatons, but they can't figure out how to fill their stomachs."

Maia smiled politely at the woman. She was clearly upset by the tone of Nate's response.

"Um, hi, I'm Maia."

"Oh jeez, I'm forgetting myself. Maia, this is Atalanta, the 'woman' your dad was talking about. She's a member of our crew."

Maia noticed a flicker of nervousness when Nate spoke. "Are you two dating?"

"Oh, c'mon Maia."

"Dating? No! I am an Argonaut, not some man's prize," said Atalanta, her eyes firing daggers at Maia.

Maia stifled a laugh. She wasn't sure why she found the tension between Nate and Atalanta so funny. She racked her brain for some information about Atalanta, but if she knew her story she'd forgotten it. Her memory of Greek mythology was clouded when she was in Olympia, and it frustrated her greatly. Except, she remembered the Golden Fleece. That's odd, thought Maia.

"*Ahem*," muttered Nate. "Atalanta joined the Argonauts a short time after my father died. He wouldn't have been okay with a woman in our ranks. He was afraid it'd be too much of a distraction."

"That is ridiculous," spat Atalanta. "I have taken an oath of virginity to the goddess Artemis."

Maia sucked in and bit her bottom lip to keep from laughing. Nate cut his eyes sideways, silently pleading with Maia to get a hold of herself. Maia cleared her throat and managed a toothless grin. Atalanta looked back and forth between Nate and Maia. Finally, she stomped off in the direction of the stables.

"Thanks a lot for that. Atalanta is very special, and she's been an invaluable member of our crew."

"Special in what way?" Maia asked.

"Maybe she'll give you a demonstration later. Look, there are still a few things we should talk about... Maia?"

But Maia was otherwise occupied. Not far off, Captain Penelopeia had emerged from a tent. She spoke quickly to a pair of Amazons and marched off.

"You know what, Nate, I would love to keep catching up, but I have to talk to someone. I'll find you later," said Maia before running after Captain Penelopeia.

Maia caught up to the captain outside of Queen Hippolyta's tent. "Captain! I've been looking for you. Where have you been?"

Captain Penelopeia turned toward Maia but couldn't seem to meet her eyes.

"Captain, are you alright?"

"I was just given an accounting of those lost while I was in the homeworld," said Captain Penelopeia in a gravelly tone. "Kore will not travel alone to the realm of Hades."

"She died with honor," offered Maia.

The captain nodded. "It is good to see you in your armor."

"It feels apt, given what we face," said Maia, straightening her gauntlets. "Captain Penelopeia, I need to know what we're doing to get Jordi back."

"Your brother will be returned safely. I promise you that."

"That's what everyone keeps saying, but... Nate and the Argonauts came up empty. There's no trace of Circe anywhere. We're stuck waiting for Dorian and Icarus to come back. What if they don't have any news either?"

Captain Penelopeia put her hand on Maia's shoulder. "Put your trust in Queen Hippolyta."

"I do trust her, as I trust you and all of my sisters."

"Good." Captain Penelopeia turned on her heel and walked in the direction of the armory.

That was disappointing, thought Maia. Despite their reassurances, Maia believed that Queen Hippolyta and Captain Penelopeia were as discouraged as was she. And they were not much better at hiding it. Maia pulled her sword from its sheath, spinning it in her hand. A vision of Akantha appeared before her eyes, and Maia stabbed the air. She needed to release some energy.

Maia ducked behind a tent. She'd been ordered by her father to stay within the confines of the invisible shroud, but Amazons only take orders from their queen – at least that's how Maia justified her plan to explore the countryside. She sprinted away from the tent, disappearing within a grove of fig trees. Her lips curled back. The shroud had to be close.

Maia stepped gingerly through the trees, branches cracking beneath her feet. She looked back at the camp. She was far enough away that she could probably chop down a tree without alerting anyone. But then, not far ahead, came a pair of voices. Maia ducked to the ground. Ten yards beyond the grove, the landscape appeared to shimmer, and Dorian stepped into view followed by Icarus.

"I beg to differ," said Dorian.

"My father agrees with me."

"I hate to break it to you, but your father is an ass."

"Yes, I know," said Icarus. "Why does everyone insist on reminding me of that?"

Maia picked herself up, brushing dirt from her knees. "What news do you bring?"

"Maia, where did you come from?" asked Dorian.

"Long Island," Maia answered, her eyes in a thin line. "Please tell me you found out something about where Circe is keeping Jordi."

Dorian and Icarus exchanged quick glances.

"We cannot be certain," said Dorian, "but all evidence points to Mount Olympus. As expected, Circe has claimed Zeus's throne. Your brother must be there as well."

"Mount Olympus," Maia repeated. "How do we get there?"

"That, unfortunately, will not be—"

"My father will know a way," interrupted Icarus. "He will be here soon."

"Today just keeps getting better and better," said Maia.

* * *

DAEDALUS SLAMMED HIS HAND DOWN on the table. Maia met his gaze with a vigorous stink-eye. She held a remarkable level of hatred for someone she'd only had the misfortune of meeting twice before.

"We must abandon Olympia," said Daedalus. "There is no other recourse."

"And where would you have us go?" asked Dorian.

Daedalus looked as if a foul smell had passed beneath his nose. "To the homeworld," he said.

"That would not be wise for many, many reasons," countered Dorian, "the least of all being we cannot allow Circe to have free reign over Olympia."

"She already does. There is no reason to discuss this further. An assault on Mount Olympus is futile."

Maia looked at the group gathered around the table one by one. She imagined her father was using everything in his power to remain calm, but he could scarcely hide his contempt for Daedalus. Dorian kept his head in motion as if juggling a heavy crown. Icarus's hand trembled as he reached for a goblet of water. Queen Hippolyta sat stone-faced, barely acknowledging Daedalus. Nate's expression was the best – he looked bored, and he made no effort to stifle a yawn.

Maia glared at Daedalus. "And what about my brother?"

"Who are you again?"

Maia jumped to her feet. "I'm the one who's going to kick your ass from here to Mount Olympus, you pompous piece of—"

"Maia! That is enough," said her father.

"Are you kidding me? We're just going to sit here while he—"

"Quite right, Maia," interrupted Queen Hippolyta. "We have sat here long enough. Daedalus, your prior service warrants you a seat at this table, but I caution you not to disrespect Maia again. If the child is on Mount Olympus, then our mission is clear. Send a message when you are prepared to do more than talk. Maia, would you please accompany me?"

The men, save for Daedalus, stood as the queen rose.

Maia's cheeks burned. She met eyes with Icarus, giving him a curt smile before pushing past Dorian to follow Queen Hippolyta. Nate reached out to take her hand, but she pulled her arm away.

"I'll find you later," Maia mumbled. She stood next to Queen Hippolyta. The queen nodded and turned her back to the men around the table.

"I find it best in moments such as this to try to break something," said Queen Hippolyta.

"Your majesty?"

"Would you care to spar?"

The edges of Maia's mouth tucked up. "Yeah, I think I need that."

"You do not care much for Daedalus?"

"Is it that obvious?"

Queen Hippolyta's mouth rested in a faint smile.

"He's just a phenomenal jerk," said Maia. "Not once did he make mention or even acknowledge that Circe has Jordi. I can't believe my father just sat there."

"Your father is quite adept at remaining motionless," said Queen Hippolyta. "I would imagine Matthias's thoughts are aligned with mine. Daedalus's opinions are worthless, but he is more knowledgeable about the inner workings of Olympia than most of us. He may help us secure access to Mount Olympus."

Queen Hippolyta stopped in front of the armory. A guard nodded and pulled open the flap to the tent. "Now, shall we find a means for redirecting our aggression?"

Maia pushed her hair out of her face and behind her ears. "Do you promise to go easy on me?"

"No," said Queen Hippolyta, entering the armory.

"Good," said Maia.

CHAPTER THIRTEEN

HER SPECIAL TALENT

MAIA COLLAPSED TO THE FLOOR OF HER TENT.

"Ow," she mumbled. "Ow, ow, ow."

Maia rolled onto her back, her eyes focusing on a small hole in the ceiling of the tent. She lifted her hand, imagining she could plug the hole with her finger, but she was met with a sharp pain in her shoulder. Groaning, Maia let her hand fall to her side.

"Maia? Are you in there?"

Maia pressed her lips together.

"Maia?"

"Yes, I'm here," said Maia, dragging herself up into a sitting position.

Icarus pushed his way through the tent flap. "I came to... Maia! Are you injured?"

"I'm fine," Maia answered. "I was just, um, working out with the queen."

Icarus kneeled beside her. "Are you sure?"

"Yes," said Maia, arching her back. "It was needed."

"Because of my father," said Icarus.

"Is that a question or a statement?"

Icarus pulled his lips into a straight line.

"He's kind of a dick," said Maia.

"My father is... well-intentioned," said Icarus. "He will help rescue your brother."

"I think I'll take that with about a million grains of salt. He doesn't give the impression he cares about anyone but himself."

Icarus seemed keen to counter Maia's claim, but he clamped his mouth shut.

"Did you want something?" asked Maia.

Icarus's entire body tensed. "I wanted to make sure you were well."

"Thank you. I'm fine."

"Then I will allow you to rest," said Icarus. He bowed and backed out of the tent.

Maia fell onto her side, pulling her knees up into her chest. She didn't think she'd ever been so ready for someone to leave. But then she felt an electric shock of guilt. Icarus wasn't to blame for his father's arrogance. Maia straightened out her legs and rolled onto her stomach. She pushed herself onto her knees and into a squatting position. Every muscle in her legs vibrated. With a last gasp, she stood and stretched.

"Am I interrupting something?" asked Nate, poking his head into the tent.

Maia tilted her head. "Yes, I was just about to take a bubble bath."

Nate's cheeks turned a light shade of pink. "Well, then, I guess I'll leave you to it."

Maia exhaled. "I was actually going to go apologize to Icarus."

Nate's fingers grazed the side of the tent flap as he entered. "What for?"

Maia felt a quiet throb of excitement at being alone again with Nate. She closed her eyes tightly and focused on her breath. "I took my anger with his father out on him."

"I reckon he's used to that."

"You, on the other hand, seem way too pleased with yourself."

"Damn, firecracker. So, after you chase Icarus down to apologize, will I be next?"

"I just mean that you seem to be enjoying this whole situation."

Nate raised his eyebrows. "Well, if that isn't the most hilarious statement ever. What could I possibly be enjoying about this? If that little confab back there proved anything it's that we're still spinning our wheels. You want to push me away, Maia? Well, go ahead. But treating me and Icarus like trash isn't going to get your brother back any sooner."

Maia grabbed Nate's arm before he could push his way out of the tent. "Wait, please! Nate, I'm sorry. I am so... freaking sorry."

Nate shook his head as he turned to face Maia. "I get it. You're scared and frustrated. It all seems hopeless. I feel the same way, but we have to stick together."

Maia swallowed thickly. "I know. I swear, if I ever make it to college, I could earn a degree in biting the heads off the people who care about me the most."

Nate wrapped his arms around Maia, and she rested her head on his arm. They were both quiet. Nate sniffed, and Maia looked up at him.

"I really am sorry," said Maia.

"It's okay."

"No, it's not."

Nate ran his fingers through Maia's hair. "You can make it up to me."

Maia pulled herself free from Nate. "I'm not that easy."

"Aw, jeez, Maia, will you relax? And I'm not that hard up either. I want you to talk to Atalanta."

"What? Why?"

"She started acting funny when we got to camp. I just spoke to her, and she's, well, not herself. I think it has something to do with you."

Maia poked Nate in the cheek. "And you said not everything in this place revolves around me."

"It doesn't," said Nate, grinning back at Maia, "or at least I don't think so. But I trust her. If she needs to speak to you, it must be important."

"Do I get to see her 'special' talent?"

"If you're lucky."

* * *

UNDER THE PINK TWILIGHT SKY, Maia scanned the outskirts of camp for a tree with golden apples. Nate said Atalanta would await her there. Maia passed many trees before finding the one Nate had described. Its gilded leaves shimmered, and the apples it bore appeared to have been placed by King Midas, he of the golden touch. Something told Maia not to touch the fruit. She sat against the tree and peered up between its branches. If the gods wanted her to have an apple, then the gods would provide one.

Maia poked a root of the tree with a stick. Where was Atalanta, and what was so pressing that she needed to see Maia without delay? Maia threw the stick several yards away. She felt movement beneath her, and she shifted her seat, fearing she'd sat on an ant-hill. Above her, the branches of the tree quivered. The ground shook as if a train were approaching.

Whoosh!

Maia pushed her hair away from her face. The gust of wind that accompanied the noise stopped as quickly as it began. The ground settled, and Maia scanned her immediate area. The stick she'd thrown was snapped in two. Maia walked over and picked up the pieces. There was a footprint in the dirt where the stick had been broken.

Again, the ground shook.

Whoosh!

The pieces of the stick were gone! In their place was a golden apple. And standing under the apple tree was Atalanta.

"You should have a bite. They taste as good as they look," said Atalanta.

"That was you? You did... all that," Maia choked. "Were you running?"

"The gods blessed me with great speed." Atalanta plucked an apple. "You should try it."

Maia bit into the apple. Its succulent juices trickled down her chin. She'd barely swallowed when she took three more bites in rapid succession. "This is – *chomp!* – incredible."

"I told you," said Atalanta, tossing an apple core onto a pile of six others.

"You eat as quickly as you run."

"I need to replenish. Running takes quite a bit out of me."

Maia finished her apple and added the core to Atalanta's pile.

"Nate thought we should talk. I was surprised."

"If I seemed uncomfortable earlier, it is only because I find it much easier to speak outside the company of men."

"So, why'd you join up with an all-boy band?"

Atalanta sucked her lips into an even line. "I did not have much choice in the matter. After my beloved, Hippomenes, was transformed into a lion—"

"By Circe?"

"By the goddess Cybele."

"I never heard of her."

"Then perhaps you know of the goddess of love, Aphrodite. She accused Hippomenes of failing to sufficiently honor her for the part she played in our union. Aphrodite tricked us into having sex in Cybele's temple, and Cybele cursed him. She turned my lover into a beast. I tried to tame Hippomenes, but... he is lost to me. I had outrun countless men who pursued me, but I loved Hippomenes. And I will never love another. With a heavy heart, I rededicated myself to Artemis, goddess of the wilderness. After Heracles in his madness destroyed the woods where I made my home, I was adrift until I joined Captain Nathaniel and his men aboard their ship, the *Argo*."

Maia scratched at her eyebrow. "The Amazons would be a better fit if you ask me."

"Would they have me?

Maia tipped her palms up. "I can't speak for the entire tribe, but I'd think someone with your *talent* would be an asset."

Atalanta plucked another apple, devouring it in seconds. "I must confess that is my desire. Captain Nathaniel has been most welcoming, but there are times when I feel so utterly out of place. I thought perhaps you could help me in making an overture to the queen."

"I can certainly try. What about Nate?"

"I am most displeased at the prospect of angering him. You know him better than I. Do you think—"

"I'm not so sure I do know him better," interrupted Maia.

"But you would like to?"

"What?"

Atalanta's cheeks went pink. "Forgive me, but I thought the two of you... "

"Slow down there. I'm not in the right state of mind to be thinking of Nate as anything but an ally in finding my brother."

"That's a shame. He is quite taken with you."

Maia felt her own face take on a crimson hue. "And how do you know that?"

"I overheard him speaking with Tydeus," said Atalanta.

"In homeroom?"

Atalanta cocked her head. "I beg your pardon?"

Maia waved her hand. "Forget it. That's very nice and all—"

"But the safe return of your brother is the priority. I will say no more."

"I'll see if I can speak to Queen Hippolyta for you," said Maia. "How fast can you run?"

Atalanta beamed. "I have never measured properly, but I suspect I am faster than a leopard. My speed proved very helpful as a member of the crew of the *Argo*. Once, I had to outrun a centaur."

"That's something you don't see everyday."

"That is something you will not see again. The last of the centaurs was killed by Circe's forces weeks ago."

"I think there might still be a couple at the San Diego Zoo," said Maia.

"I do not understand. What is a 'zoo'?"

"Sorry. I get my appreciation for corny jokes from my father. He developed the ability to use 'dad humor' pretty quickly for someone who was frozen as a statue for millennia."

"Yes, well," said Atalanta, smiling politely, "perhaps your father would enjoy an apple. And your mother as well. In fact, I will pick them all."

There was a blur of activity around the tree. Within seconds, Atalanta had robbed it of all its fruit.

"Here," said Maia, "let me take some of those. I can't imagine we'll find worms in any of them. Say, that reminds me. Have you ever seen an amphisbaena?"

"No, and I pray to the gods I never do. I would not mind if Circe destroyed every last one."

Maia could make out a sliver of her bracelet behind her armful of apples. The first two symbols to appear on her bracelet made sense. The wings represented her flight with Icarus. The sword signified her induction into the sisterhood of the Amazons. Maia shuddered to think what fate had in store for her with a poison-spouting, two-headed snake.

"There are some, however," said Atalanta, "who believe keeping an amphisbaena around your neck ensures a safe pregnancy."

"I'll keep that in mind if things work out with Nate."

"I do not... Oh, is that more of the 'dad humor' to which you referred?"

"Actually, I don't think my dad would find that funny at all."

CHAPTER FOURTEEN

NOWHERE TO HIDE

MAIA LAUGHED SO HARD that several apples tumbled out of her arms onto the rocky terrain.

"You're telling me that Nate – *Ha! Ha!* – drove the boat right into the rocks? After telling you that you should leave the steering to him?" asked Maia. "Oh, man, that's awesome."

Atalanta chuckled. "Well, in all fairness, I do not think he was questioning my abilities so much as he was trying to impress the men. He had rather large shoes to fill after his father died."

Maia stooped to pick up an apple. "Yeah, I'm sure it was tough." Maia silently cursed at herself. She'd barely acknowledged that Nate had lost his father. After all the grief she'd given him for keeping secrets, it was Maia that was the lousy friend.

"Did you know his father?" asked Atalanta.

"No, I've never met anyone from Nate's family. Back home, he lives on the other side of the country. Before today, I hadn't seen Nate in two years."

"He was pleased to see you."

"For someone who's taken an oath of virginity, you seem to enjoy playing matchmaker."

Atalanta's cheeks went red. "I merely wish to see my captain happy."

"Yes, well—"

BOOM! BOOM!

"What the hell was that?" asked Maia, her eyes darting about.

BOOM! BOOM! BOOM!

"Something is hitting the shroud. Look!"

In the distance, past the tree that'd held the golden apples, waves of iridescent light appeared in the sky. The protective shroud was buckling under some enormous pressure.

BOOM! BOOM!

"I have to find my parents," said Maia, dropping the apples and sprinting to the center of the camp where the Amazons had built a bonfire. All around, her sisters were donning armor and gathering weapons.

"To arms, sisters, to arms!" cried Captain Penelopeia. "We have little time."

"Captain! Have you seen my parents?" asked Maia.

"No, sister, I have not, but you would be wise to arm yourself. The shroud will not withstand much more. Once it falls, the camp will be overrun with Circe's abominations."

BOOM! BOOM! BOOM!

"What's hitting the shroud?"

Captain Penelopeia ran off before she could answer. Maia stood with her back to the bonfire. Chaos unfolded before her eyes. Amazons on horseback charged past her. In their hurry to arm themselves, the Amazons, along with the Argonauts, were knocking tents to the ground and scattering weapons. Maia picked up a shield. Her sword was safely secured to her belt.

BOOM! BOOM!

As she ran past Maia, an Amazon pointed to the sky. Maia turned in time to see a massive fist strike the shroud.

BOOM!

"What the—"

"Maia! Thank goodness you're safe!" called her father as he ran toward her.

"What is that?" asked Maia.

"A Cyclops. More than one, I'd imagine. The shroud won't hold. We have to leave."

"Where's Mom?"

"She's with Queen Hippolyta. She's safe for now."

Maia silently agreed. There was no one in camp she'd rather have her mother being watched over by.

"Dad, if we leave, there's bound to be hybrids out there. It's getting dark. How are we going to get past them?" asked Maia.

Matthias kneeled and held her hands. "We've been preparing for this moment. I don't know what's waiting for us out there, but we're going to get through. We're going to find your brother, and we're going home."

"Dad—"

"Maia, whatever happens, you have to go to Varkiza. That's where we'll meet up if we get separated. The *Argo* is docked there."

"But we traveled north from Varkiza before crossing the barrier. Why didn't we just—"

BOOM! BOOM! CRASH!

"The shroud is coming apart. We have to hurry," said Matthias as he grabbed her by the wrist. "We have to get your mother."

Maia and her father dashed through the camp. The cries of her sisters filled the air, buoyed by the sound of horses and wagons rushing past them. A collective scream went out, signaling that the shroud was no more. In place of the thundering thuds of the fists pounding the shroud was a guttural chorus of roars that cut the air. The Cyclopes had penetrated the camp!

Maia followed her father to the rear of Queen Hippolyta's tent. There stood the queen, with Maia's mother next to her. They were flanked by two of the largest Amazons Maia had ever seen.

"Mom!" Maia cried, running into her mother's open arms.

"Thank you, your highness," said Matthias.

"*RAAAAAAARRRRGGHHHHHH!*"

Queen Hippolyta's tent was ripped away. Looming over the group was a giant with one massive eye in the center of its forehead. The queen's guards nodded at each other and rushed the Cyclops, their swords at the ready.

"Let's move!" yelled Matthias.

Maia and her father each grabbed her mother by an arm and ran past the Cyclops. Maia looked over her shoulder. Queen Hippolyta joined her guards in dealing the beast blow after blow.

"*RAAAAAAARRRRGGHHHHHH!*"

"This way!" shouted Matthias. "We have to get up that hill."

"Matt, I can't see where we're going!" cried Eleanor.

"Hang on, my love. We'll get to safety. I promise."

Her father's words had barely left his mouth when Maia was struck from behind. She fell to the ground, losing her grip on her mother in the process. Maia rolled onto her back, holding her shield in front of her.

"Maia!" cried Matthias. "Maia, where are you?"

"I'm over—" Maia began, but she fell silent as something rammed into her shield. A claw scratched against her chin. Maia kicked her legs out, making contact with her assailant. She reached for her sword and swung it blindly.

Maia felt something solid hit her arm, and her sword went flying. She scrambled to her feet and ran, but she was knocked down again after several yards. Hands grabbed her under her arms, and for a brief moment she felt as if she was flying through the air. Hitting the ground, she picked herself up to her hands and knees, but a snarling beast put a foot on her back and drove her down. Maia winced in pain.

THUD!

The foot was gone. A flash of light filled Maia's vision.

"Are you okay?" asked Nate, holding a torch in one hand and a sword in the other.

"*GAAAHHH!*"

In the light of the torch, Maia could see the creature that had overtaken her. It was part man, part wolf, and it lay on the ground bleeding. Two of Nate's men pulled their swords from its corpse.

"I'm so glad we found you," said Nate.

"My parents!" cried Maia. "They were in front of me. They were headed for a hill."

"It's alright. We'll find them. Can you get up?"

Maia pushed herself off the ground. As she steadied herself, a familiar gust of wind swept past her.

"Captain, the woods are crawling with unimaginable beasts," said Atalanta.

"Oh, I can imagine alright," said Nate. "We need to find Maia's parents."

"It is impossible to see anything."

"They were right next to me," said Maia. "How far could they have gotten?"

"Let's head up that ridge," said Nate, handing Maia a sword. "Your father was probably trying to get your mother out of harm's way."

The meaning behind Nate's words hit Maia like a ton of bricks. Of course her father would keep going. He trusted Maia to take care of herself. Her mother, on the other hand, was scarcely equipped to deal with this mayhem.

Maia ran alongside Nate, the cries of battle all around them. As they charged up the hill where Maia hoped to find her parents, they came face to face with a pack of Circe's hybrids. Maia tucked and rolled, cutting the legs out from under two of the beasts. One of the Argonauts threw a spear, catching another creature in the throat. Atalanta sped around them, bashing the remaining beasts with the gnarled branch of a tree. The group bounded over the beasts, and crested the hill.

"Dad! Mom!" yelled Maia. "Where are you?"

No answer came.

"They must've kept going."

"My father said to meet in Varkiza if we got separated," said Maia.

"Yes, that's the plan. We've figured out a way to get to Mount Olympus," said Nate.

"But how do we get to Varkiza?"

"We follow the stars, firecracker. That's the same way your parents are going to get there."

"It seems like there are so few of us," said Maia.

"Some of the Argonauts left before sundown. I reckon the Amazons are fighting the Cyclopes, trying to give the rest of us a head start."

"Does everyone know to go to Varkiza?"

"Icarus knows. I'm sure Dorian will head there too if he tries to go back to camp. He left shortly after you and the queen bolted from the meeting. He was trying to get in touch with his son, Triton. He had to find a—"

"Water source," interrupted Maia.

"Exactly."

Not too far in the distance, Maia heard the galloping of horses, followed by further shouting and the clashing of weaponry. More of Circe's beasts lay ahead of them.

Maia ran in the direction of the conflict. In the moonlight, she saw a trio of Amazons tearing into a pack of hybrids. Nate jumped into the fray, slicing the head off a beast with the lower body of an ape. Maia threw her shield to one of the Amazons, just in time to block the jaws of a creature the original parts of which Maia couldn't decipher. She skidded next to Nate and cut down another of the hybrids.

"Thank you, sister," said an Amazon.

"HOUYHNHNM!"

A few feet away lay a horse, its stomach clawed open. One of the Amazons kneeled beside it, whispering words of comfort before ending its suffering with the tip of her sword. Maia watched the animal take its last breath.

"We have to keep going," said Nate, touching Maia's arm. "It's going to be a long night."

Maia looked Nate in the eyes. "Thank you for saving me back there. I thought I was—"

"Stop. You're welcome."

"I'm glad you're here."

"So, all is forgiven?"

"As long as you forgive me for being such a jerk."

Nate wrapped his arms around Maia. "It's all good, firecracker. And I'm glad you're here too."

"If you and 'firecracker' are done, we need to go," said Atalanta before speeding off.

"I told you she was special," said Nate.

"She told me that you nearly wrecked the ship when you first took over."

"Did I also mention that she's a horrible liar?"

"I had a few sailing lessons when I was younger," said Maia. "If you want, I'll be the captain."

"And here I wondered why my father didn't want women on the crew."

CHAPTER FIFTEEN

LITTLE MORE THAN BUGS

MAIA STACKED THE LAST of the brown cardboard boxes in the flatbed of her father's truck. In permanent marker, she wrote her initials next to a smiley face. There were over fifty boxes, some the size of a matchbox, while others were bigger than a microwave oven.

RUMBLE RUMBLE

One of the boxes was moving. It was smaller than most. Maia climbed onto the flatbed and reached for the box.

RUMBLE RUMBLE

The box continued to shake, moving beyond Maia's reach. She cleared some boxes out of the way, climbing on others. Maia was able to graze the corner of the box with her pinky.

RUMBLE RUMBLE CRASH!

The box fell off the truck, landing on the sidewalk below. Maia scooted down from the boxes and jumped from the flatbed. The box continued to shake, moving under the truck. Maia fell to her knees and grabbed the box from behind the rear tire. It stopped shaking. Maia turned the box over. Written on the side of the box were the letters 'JMP'.

"Jordi Maxwell Peterson," said Maia. She pulled at the tape sealing the box and opened its flaps. Maia tore aside old newsprint and removed an object from the box. It was a wind-up tin soldier with a tall red hat and jacket holding a musket. The soldier had a large brass heart-shaped key sticking out of its back. Maia turned the key, and it snapped off in her hand.

"Oh no, what have you done?" asked a voice from behind Maia. It was her neighbor Mrs. Tuttle.

"The key broke off. I'm sure I can fix it," said Maia, poking the key back into the soldier.

"How could you let this happen to your brother? Your parents are going to be so upset!" cried Mrs. Tuttle.

"It's just a toy," said Maia.

"A toy? How can you be so callous?" asked Mrs. Tuttle, tears streaming down her face. "Oh, poor Jordi! He'll never be the same!"

"Stop! This isn't Jordi! It's a stupid tin toy. Jordi is perfectly... " Maia stopped.

"Perfectly what, dear? You don't know, do you?" asked Mrs. Tuttle. "YOU DON'T KNOW ANYTHING!"

Maia ran from Mrs. Tuttle, cradling the toy soldier in her arms. She turned the corner of her block and ran toward Memorial Park. In place of the benches, there stood a long table surrounded by chairs tied with balloons. Her parents were positioned behind the table, and her father was holding a large sheet cake. Strung between two trees was a banner with the words 'HAPPY BIRTHDAY, JORDI!'

Maia stopped at the entrance to the park. Her mother waved at her to join them, but Maia remained motionless. The toy soldier stirred. Maia looked down. The soldier was gone. She was holding Jordi. He was wearing light blue footie pajamas with golden stars.

"You can let him go," said her father.

"No!" yelled Maia. "I have to keep him safe."

"It's okay, sweetie," said her mother. "Let him go."

Maia opened her arms, and Jordi floated up and away. He became smaller and smaller until he vanished in a blink of light. Maia looked for her parents, but they were no longer in the park. The sky turned black with streaks of red. Maia took a step toward the table. Most of the balloons were gone, and the tablecloth was stained and ripped. At the end of the table was the sheet cake. Next to the cake rested a knife. Maia picked it up and cut into the cake. A trickle of blood seeped from the cake, and Maia threw the knife to the ground.

"This is just a dream," cried Maia. "This is just a dream! WAKE UP!"

Maia bolted up from the ground... and out of her dream. "JORDI!"

"Hey firecracker, it's okay! You must've had a nightmare," said Nate, putting his arm around Maia.

"Where am I?" asked Maia, running her hand across her chest. She was drenched with sweat. Sighing, Maia dropped to her knees.

"You fell asleep. I did, too," said Nate. "We stopped to rest. We'd been going all night, and we seemed to be out of the woods."

Maia sat back on the soles of her feet. She rubbed the sleep out of her eyes. The sun glimmered through the branches of a fig tree. Memories of the previous night came flooding into her mind. She, Nate, and Atalanta had fled the Amazon's camp with two Amazons – Io and Eurybia – and two Argonauts – Augeas and Telamon. They'd encountered more of Circe's creatures than she could count, but they'd survived until sunrise. They'd stopped in a grove of fig trees, and exhaustion had claimed Maia.

"How far are we from Varkiza?" asked Maia.

"To be honest, I'm not sure. Atalanta is out trying to get the lay of the land. Eurybia and Telamon are still asleep. Io and Augeas are looking for water."

"There's no one else around?"

Nate shook his head. "We seem to be the only ones. I don't know what happened back at camp. There were at least three Cyclopes... and tons of other creatures. The Amazons had their hands full."

Maia pictured the funeral pyre after the Amazons had clashed with Heracles and his forces two years ago, but quickly pushed it out of her mind.

"You okay, firecracker?"

"No. Are you?"

"I'll be better when we get to Varkiza," replied Nate. "Your parents will be there. I'm certain of it."

"It doesn't make sense. Even if my father had kept running to get my mother out of danger, we should've crossed paths with them. It's almost like... "

Nate squinted his eyes. "What?"

"Like one of the hybrids threw me far away from them," finished Maia. "I know it sounds strange, but—"

"Strange is relative in this place," interrupted Nate. "I'm just glad we found you when we did."

CRACK!

"Someone's coming," said Maia, reaching for her sword. A moment later, Io and Augeas came around a tree holding plump leather waterskins.

"Captain," said Augeas, nodding. "There is a stream not far from here."

"Great, thanks," said Nate, reaching for a waterskin. He held it out to Maia.

"Thank you," said Maia before taking a swig. "If we're near a stream, maybe we can contact Dorian."

"Do you know how to do that?" asked Nate, taking the water-skin back from Maia.

"It's worth a try," said Maia, getting to her feet. "How are you, Io?"

"I am better than I could hope, sister," replied Io, lifting the side of her tunic. A bloodied swath of cloth barely managed to cover a deep cut she'd sustained during the night.

"That looks bad," said Maia, sucking in her breath.

"I will manage," said Io, covering up her wound. She turned and drank from a waterskin as she walked toward a large rock. Wiping her chin, Io sat on the ground in front of the rock, leaned back, and closed her eyes.

"Captain, has Atalanta returned?" asked Augeas.

"Not yet," replied Nate. "She's been gone a while. Too long, in fact, especially for her."

"Are you worried?" asked Maia.

Nate smiled. "Not anymore," he said, cocking his head and pointing past Maia.

The ground shook as Atalanta ran to Nate's side, trailed by a gust of wind. Maia swept her hair out of her face.

"Did you have any luck?" asked Nate.

"We are but a few hours from Varkiza," answered Atalanta. "Shorter than that for me, of course."

"Of course," repeated Nate. "Did you see anyone else?"

"No, Captain."

"Alright then, go find Eurybia and Telamon and tell them we're heading out," said Nate. "Augeas, which way is the stream? We should get more water. And, Maia, if you want to try to contact Dorian, I guess it's worth a shot."

"I will escort Maia to the stream," said Atalanta. "I know where it is."

"Alright, we'll catch up with you," said Nate. "Be careful. There's no telling what or who you might find out there."

* * *

NO WORDS WERE EXCHANGED between Maia and Atalanta as they headed for the stream. Maia could think of little else than the circumstances that'd caused her to become separated from her parents. *Strange is relative*, Nate had said, and Maia could scarcely think of anything more true in Olympia. Speaking of strange, Atalanta kept sneaking sideway glances at Maia, turning away before Maia could meet her eyes.

"Did you sleep at all?" asked Maia.

"No."

"Do you sleep?"

"I am blessed with great speed, but I am a mortal. And even the gods sleep."

"Not according to my father."

Atalanta stopped. "That is nonsense."

Maia raised her eyebrows. "You seem pretty confident in your knowledge of the gods."

"I have no reason not to be confident. I was a most faithful servant."

"But no longer?"

"Few gods remain, and those who do are a cowardly lot. Do you not agree?"

"That's not a word I would have used, but I guess after Aphrodite—"

"DO NOT SPEAK HER NAME!" interrupted Atalanta, her hands gesticulating wildly. "Do you know what the goddess of love took from me? Do you have any idea what it was like to have my beloved stripped away so cruelly?"

"I'm sure it was—"

"Bugs! The gods treated us as little more than bugs," said Atalanta, as she sat under an olive tree, a few feet below an intricately woven spider web. "Do you know the story of Arachne?"

"Do you mean her contest with Athena?"

"Yes! Athena, so-called goddess of war and wisdom, was so jealous of Arachne's skills at weaving that she forced her into a contest to see who could weave the greatest tapestry. And, when it was obvious that Arachne – *'a mere mortal'* – was the more talented of the two, Athena beat her within an inch of her life before transforming her into a spider. Did she deserve that?"

"Atalanta, I think we should—"

"I am glad Circe took Lord Zeus's throne," hissed Atalanta.

"That's enough!" yelled Maia, her hand finding the hilt of her sword. "Circe has my brother. I don't care how angry you are with the gods. If you speak that way again, I won't hesitate to—"

"To what?" asked Atalanta, her knees bashing against each other. "What could you possibly take from me that I have not already lost?"

Before Maia could say another word, Atalanta was standing in front of her. Maia lifted her sword, but Atalanta knocked it away.

"There is someone who wants to see you," said Atalanta, grabbing Maia and lifting her over her shoulder with her god-granted speed. There was a rush of air as Atalanta sped off with Maia. A few seconds passed, and Atalanta stopped, throwing Maia to the ground in the process.

"What do you think you're doing?" asked Maia, choking on the dust kicked up when she fell. "Are you insane? I trusted you. Nate trusted you."

"The captain will understand," said Atalanta, her voice cracking. "There was no other way. I had to get you alone."

"It was you last night," said Maia, getting to her feet. "You took me away from my parents. If you hurt them, I swear—"

"They are uninjured. Your parents are on their way to Varkiza. But it does not matter. You will not see them again."

"Atalanta, you don't have to do this. Take me back to Nate, and we'll work it out. Nobody has to come to any harm."

"It is too late for that," said Atalanta, thrusting her chin past Maia.

Maia turned around. Several yards away, hanging by a rope from a pair of trees were the lifeless bodies of Eurybia and Telamon.

"No!" cried Maia, running toward them. "What have you done?"

Maia fell to her knees and closed her eyes. This is not how it ends, she thought to herself. Looking up, Maia saw that Eurybia's sword still hung from the sheath on her belt. She bolted toward the tree and kicked off it, knocking into Eurybia and clutching her fallen sister's blade before it hit the charred soil.

"That will do you no good," said Atalanta. "Put down the sword."

"And why would I do that?"

Cackling laughter filled the air, and Maia gulped down a breath. Akantha, disgraced Amazon and daughter of Circe, stepped from behind a tree.

"Because you have already lost."

CHAPTER SIXTEEN

THE FALLEN PRINCESS

AKANTHA PUSHED TELAMON'S BOOT, causing his corpse to sway ever so slightly. Her lips curled back into a sickening grin.

"Shame, really. He was quite handsome," said Akantha. "But not as attractive as the son of Jason. After I am done with you, I will get to know him better."

"Where's my brother?" hissed Maia.

"The boy? Oh, I left him somewhere. I am sure he is quite all right. Aeton offered to watch him."

"Akantha, if you've hurt him, I swear I will—"

"Oh, shut your mouth. You will do nothing, except perhaps to bleed."

Maia raised Eurybia's sword, but Atalanta grabbed it and hurled it beyond the tree line. Maia stepped forward, and Atalanta whizzed past her and knocked her to the ground.

"Why are you helping her? She's crazy!" said Maia.

"She will give me back my love," said Atalanta, the words barely escaping her lips.

"You can't believe her!"

"Quiet! She has promised to return Hippomenes to human form," said Atalanta. "Is that not right, my mistress?"

Akantha tipped up her palms. "I may have said something about that, but really it was just conjecture. Besides, he looks much better as a lion."

Atalanta leaned forward, putting her hands on her knees. Maia thought she might throw up.

"What are you saying? You gave your word!"

"Her word is meaningless. She turned on the Amazons. She won't help you."

"It is not just that I will not. I cannot. The spell is beyond even my mother's magic," said Akantha, rubbing the large jewel in the center of a ring on her left hand. "It was cute that you believed me."

Atalanta paced back and forth, taking in huge gulps of air. "No! You will bring him back. I betrayed my captain and my crewmates. I killed for you. And I will not hesitate to kill again!"

Atalanta burst forth. Akantha opened her palm and blew a mustard-yellow powder in Atalanta's face. She fell to the ground, twisting and writhing.

"What have you done to her?" asked Maia.

"Nothing worse than what I will do to you," said Akantha.

"I don't need a sword to end this."

"Oh please, this is just the beginning. Wait until you see what my mother has cooked up."

Maia raised her fist and stepped toward Akantha.

"Now, now," said Akantha, opening her palm. "There is more where that came from."

"*Ra Ra Ooh Rao!*"

Atalanta flopped from side to side, growling and hissing.

"Excellent! Now we shall have some fun," said Akantha, gesturing to where Atalanta lay.

Maia took a tentative step backward, and then another. Atalanta continued thrashing, enveloped by a beige mist.

"*Rao!*"

The mist cleared, and Atalanta stood. Her lower body had been replaced with the hindquarters of a cheetah. Saliva dripped from her mouth. Atalanta's face was covered in spots, and she pawed wrathfully at herself.

"Well done! Oh, I just love when a transformation suits the temperament of the subject. The spots are fabulous. Do you agree?"

"You're even crazier than I thought," said Maia before running in the direction of where Eurybia's sword had landed.

"You are wasting your time," called Akantha. "Atalanta, be a dear and fetch her."

Atalanta took off after Maia as she dove through the tree line. The sword lay several yards ahead. Maia was but a few feet away when Atalanta jumped on top of her. They rolled forward, passing over the sword. Maia reached out, and her arm was swatted away. They came to a stop with Atalanta sitting on Maia's back.

Akantha came forward through the trees. "I told you."

Maia struggled to push herself off the ground, but Atalanta growled and batted her on the head. Akantha's laughter filled Maia's ears. She closed her eyes and tried to steady her breath. Atalanta was heavy, but with each breath Maia felt a tingling sensation. She pushed against the ground once more, and she felt an electric shock course through her blood. Maia threw her arms out as she lifted herself up, causing Atalanta to fly off her back. Her extraordinary strength, inherited from her father, had returned. Maia picked up Eurybia's sword.

"You were saying?"

Akantha frowned. "You really are going to make this more difficult, are you not? Fine. Have it your way." Akantha clapped her hands.

The ground began to shake and from the trees emerged two amphisbaenas. They were viler than Maia remembered. The blistered, serpentine creatures let out grotesque shrieks from each of their two heads.

"Well, go get her!" commanded Akantha.

The amphisbaenas circled around Maia, their tongues flicking in every direction. Maia raised her sword. One of the creatures struck out a head, and Maia jabbed it with her blade. The other snapped at her feet, and Maia jumped, landing a blow to its neck. Maia's eyes darted back and forth between the two amphisbaenas. They made clicking sounds to communicate with each other. Suddenly, both of the creatures lunged forward. Maia rolled backward and swung her sword, cutting off one of the heads from the beast on her right. Blood spouting from its wound, the amphisbaena screeched as it spun and twisted on the ground. Maia lunged forward and sliced off the other head.

Now for the other amphisbaena, Maia thought as she struggled to get her footing. Before she could spot the creature, she was struck from behind and fell to the ground. Maia had almost forgotten about Atalanta.

The amphisbaena that'd managed to keep both heads slid toward Maia, its tongue slicing the air. Rolling over, Maia swung her sword, striking Atalanta with the flat. She needed to incapacitate Atalanta, but still didn't want to kill her. Atalanta fell to her side. Maia picked her up and threw her at the approaching amphisbaena. Maia jumped to her feet, and bolted past the entangled pair.

"It's over, Akantha," spat Maia as she charged toward her.

"*Pffft!* Do not be ridiculous. It is not over until I say it is."

From behind Akantha popped up a pair of pincers. A set of massive eyes came into view, followed by the first of eight legs.

When the rest of the towering spider stepped out, Maia skidded to a stop.

"Do you like spiders, Maia?"

The eyes of the spider, six in number, were huge obsidian orbs. Maia caught her reflection, six versions of herself with the same grim look. She gripped her sword with both hands and steadied herself to attack.

"*Ra Ra Ooh Rao!*"

Atalanta had freed herself from the amphisbaena – ripping it apart in the process – and she crouched a few feet away. She charged forward, knocking Maia to the ground before she could block. Atalanta stood over Maia. She wiped away her drool, turned, and leapt at Akantha.

The princess, clearly startled, fell backward as the spider stepped over her. Atalanta tore past the spider's front legs but failed to dodge another pair that pinned her to the ground.

"What do you think you are doing?" screeched Akantha, stomping over to Atalanta and kicking her in the head. "You ungrateful little—"

Maia was on Akantha before she could finish her rant. She swung her sword, slicing off two of the spider's legs. The monster stumbled, but Atalanta remained trapped. Maia grabbed Akantha and threw her to the ground. "Where is he?"

"I'll never tell!"

"Then your mother will have to come looking for you," said Maia, holding her blade to Akantha's cheek. "If there's anything left of you."

The air behind Maia vibrated, and she found herself falling. She landed next to Akantha, her body covered in massive, furry fibers of webbing. Maia thrust a hand out, breaking through the vile silk, but the spider blasted her again. Maia tumbled onto her back. The monstrous spider loomed over her.

"Idiot! I told you I alone would decide when we are done here. I was going to bring you back to see your brother, but perhaps this daughter of Arachne should get to enjoy you after you chopped off two of her legs. Though it looks like she is more interested in feasting on Atalanta."

Maia pried her fingers between the giant threads. She prayed for her strength to surge again. The spider made snapping noises as its pincers edged closer and closer to Atalanta. The runner howled in pain from the leg stabbing her in the chest.

"Are you going to watch, Maia? It really is not something you see everyday, especially from where you come," said Akantha, her face overtaken by a grotesque sneer.

Thunk! Thunk! Thunk! Thunk!

Before the spider could sink its pincers into Atalanta, it was struck in four of its six eyes by arrows. It emitted a noise like a swarm of cicadas as it toppled onto its side.

Thunk! Thunk!

Another pair of arrows struck the spider in its remaining eyes. Its cries caused Maia to consider never stepping on a spider again.

"NO! NO! NO!" shrieked Akantha. "Who dares?"

Icarus dove from the sky, a pair of wings protruding from his back. He stopped in midair and kicked out his feet, knocking Akantha to the ground. Icarus landed next to Maia and pulled out a short blade. He cut through the webbing and freed Maia from the messy residue.

"Nice wings," said Maia, reaching back for her sword.

"I thought you might like them."

Maia looked past Icarus. Akantha lay face down in the dirt. "This is kind of a familiar scene."

"Well, things have a way of repeating in Olympia. Are you hurt?"

"Surprisingly not, but Atalanta doesn't look too good."

"I do not see... that is Atalanta? Did Akantha—"

"Yeah, apparently she learned a few tricks from her mother."

"More than a few, you fools," said Akantha, craning her neck. A cloud of gray smoke enveloped the princess, and when it dissipated she was gone.

Maia lunged forward, grabbing frantically at the last wisps of smoke.

Atalanta let out a low lingering growl. There was a gapping wound in her chest where the spider had her pinned. Maia grasped her sword as she approached Atalanta, but there was no need. Atalanta gave little sign of being able to breath steadily, much less attack. Her eyes were wet, and Maia too began to cry. A moment later, Atalanta was no more.

Maia plunged her sword in the gory muck created in battle. "It's not fair. She just wanted to be with her true love again."

Icarus put a hand on Maia's shoulder. She reached back with her right hand and squeezed his fingers. Maia looked around her. The spider continued to emit a death rattle, but it was motionless. The amphisbaenas were dead. And Akantha left no clue of as to where she'd escaped.

"How did you find me?" Maia asked.

"I have been searching for you since last night. I told your parents I would find you."

"Are they safe?"

"Yes. They are traveling with Queen Hippolyta to Varkiza. We will meet them there."

"We have to go back for Nate."

Icarus pulled his lips back into a straight line. "Of course."

Maia gave Icarus a hug. "Thank you. I don't know what I would have done if you hadn't shown up."

"I am sure you could have bested Akantha on your own. You have been trained well."

"Well enough, I hope, to end this."

Icarus looked Maia directly in the eye. "You are the daughter of a Titan by birth and an Amazon by your will. I have no doubt that Nike, goddess of victory, will spread her wings in your honor. If she still lives, of course. We really should keep a list of which gods are left."

Maia chuckled. "Speaking of wings, what's the story here?"

Icarus smiled. "I will tell you another time. We have company."

"Maia!" called Nate as he came sprinting. "Are you alright?"

Maia wiped the back of her hand across her forehead. "I'm unhurt."

Nate threw his arms around Maia and kissed her on the cheek. "I got so scared when you didn't come back from the stream."

Next to them, Icarus stiffened. Maia looked back and forth between Nate and Icarus. There was no time for this nonsense, she thought to herself.

"Captain!" yelled Augeas. He was standing between the bodies of Eurybia and Telamon.

Io fell to her knees in silent prayer.

"Cut them down," said Nate, shaking his head. "We'll bury them before we head out."

"And Atalanta, too," said Maia, pointing to the fallen runner.

"Circe was here?" asked Nate.

"It was Akantha," said Maia. "I don't know how to tell you this, but Atalanta tried to strike a deal with her. Atalanta killed Eurybia and Telamon. I'm sorry, but she betrayed us."

"And it looks like she paid the price. Damn, firecracker, I don't know how a world this crazy can stand."

"I just need it to last long enough to find my brother," said Maia, "and then the whole place can burn for all I care."

"You may have your wish sooner than you think," said Icarus, looking upward. Streaks of red lightning silently crisscrossed above them. Cracks seemed to form in the sky itself.

"What's happening?" asked Maia.

Icarus bowed his head. "Olympia is dying."

INTERLUDE II

WHEN MATTHIAS VANISHED

A DOOR SLAMS, AND I THROW BACK the sheets and leap out of bed. I manage to tangle my left foot in a blanket, and with a thud I hit the floor. I look back at the bed. Maia is still asleep. I creep to the door. There's shouting coming from the living room. Two of Matt's brothers are engaged in their favorite pastime – cursing at each other. Despite their volume, I can't make out what they're saying, even though I've learned to understand Greek pretty well. They're screaming over each other, and now Matt's mother joins them. She's louder than the two brothers combined. I can understand her.

Shut up before you wake Eleanor and the baby!

Another door slams, and the house is silent. It's been three weeks since Matt went out one morning and didn't come back. I've barely slept since. His brothers tell me not to worry, but they can go screw themselves. They're keeping something from me. Matt would never leave me. He wouldn't leave Maia. Something bad has happened to him.

I can hear Matt's mother crying. I don't want to be angry with her, but I need to know the truth. I slink back across the bedroom and cover Maia with the blanket. She blows a raspberry in her sleep – a habit she picked up from Matt. My heart aches for her. What if she never sees her father again?

I hear the sound of glass breaking in the living room. I edge over to the bedroom door and pull it open an inch. Matt's mother is muttering to herself as she sweeps up a broken bowl. I widen the opening ever so slightly just as the front door opens again. It's Matt's brother Dorian.

"What happened?" Dorian says in Greek.

"Your idiot brothers happened," Matt's mother responds.

Dorian crosses the living room and takes the broom and dustpan from his mother. She kisses him on the cheek.

"How's Eleanor?" asks Dorian.

"She hurts," answers Matt's mother. "How else could she be?"

They exit the living room for the kitchen, and I can't hear what they're saying.

"Dammit!" I say under my breath. I pull the bedroom open slowly and tiptoe down the hallway to the living room. Pressing up against the wall closest to the kitchen, I do my best to keep my heart from beating right out of my chest.

"He wouldn't just leave," Dorian states. "I'm worried."

"He'll be back," his mother says. "This is just like what he would do before."

"Before what?"

I hear something slam against the kitchen table.

"Enough! He would not make the journey without telling us," says Matt's mother.

Journey? Did she say *journey?* Damn it! I should've let Matt teach me more Greek. The floor creaks, and I jerk my elbow, knocking into a framed picture on the wall of Matt and his brothers. My heart nearly stops. I pause to see if Dorian or his mother heard, but there's no sound from the kitchen. I slide across the floor toward the bedroom.

"Eleanor?"

Dorian is standing in the doorway to the kitchen.

I drop my shoulders and turn to face him fully. Matt's mother pokes her head out from behind Dorian, her face ashen and beset with worry.

"Are you well?" Dorian asks in English.

I feel anger building in my core. My face is burning hot. I swallow thickly.

"No, I'm not. I'm tired. I'm hungry. I'm angry. 'Well' is nowhere on the list," I say through clenched teeth.

"I make dinner," says Matt's mother, wringing her hands on a dishcloth.

"What *journey* is Matt on?"

"I do not know what you mean," says Dorian, his face drained of color.

"You said he wouldn't make the *journey* without you," I say, straining not to yell at Matt's mother.

Her lip begins to quiver, and she buries her face in Dorian's arm.

"You are mistaken, Eleanor. We do not know where Matthias has gone," says Dorian, stroking his mother's hair.

"You're lying," I say. "You've been lying to me for weeks. You know something, and you're not telling me!"

Matt's mother is racked by sobs. Dorian whispers to her, directing her to a chair.

I cross the living room and kneel in front of her.

"I need to know the truth," I say.

Matt's mother covers her face with her hands.

"Eleanor, you must stop. There is nothing—"

"Patient," Matt's mother interrupts, staring at me with red watery eyes. "You be patient. He come back."

"I've been patient for three weeks. And now I know there's something you're keeping from me. Please! Think of Maia. What did you mean by *journey?*"

"No say *journey*," says Matt's mother. "I not know. But he come back."

"You don't know where he is, but you're so sure he'll be back," I say, shaking my head. "I can't believe you would do this to me... or to Maia."

Almost on cue, I hear Maia crying in the bedroom. I stand up and look back and forth between the two of them.

"I have to take care of my daughter."

"Eleanor, I must insist—"

"None of you are in a position to insist anything," I say before leaving the room. I kick the bedroom door closed and scoop Maia up.

"It's okay, sweetie," I lie.

Maia nuzzles her forehead against my neck.

"Somehow we're going to be okay, I promise."

CHAPTER SEVENTEEN

MISTAKES OF THE PAST

BENEATH THE FRACTURED SKY of blue and red, Maia and Nate, along with Io and Augeas, continued their trek to Varkiza. Icarus had flown ahead, which was better for all of them. He wouldn't have approved of Maia and Nate's "game". Io and Augeas didn't seem too pleased either.

"That's hardly the craziest story. Do you know the one about King Sisyphus? He cheated death, making Zeus and Hades look pretty foolish in the process. When he finally did end up in the Underworld, Sisyphus was punished by having to push a huge boulder endlessly up a steep hill."

"Yeah, and?" asked Maia.

"He could never make it to the top. Zeus made it so the boulder would roll back to the bottom of the hill, and Sisyphus had to start all over again – for an eternity."

"The gods did like their petty tortures."

"It wasn't just the gods. My dad's uncle sent him to fetch the Golden Fleece to keep him from taking back the throne he had stolen from my grandfather. He had to sail halfway across the world, fighting off harpies, sirens, and a sleepless dragon."

Maia laughed. "Why couldn't the dragon sleep?"

"Because it had to protect the Golden Fleece."

"That doesn't seem fair," said Maia, barely containing a chuckle.

"My dad got past the dragon anyway," said Nate. "What else you got?"

"Well, what's with all the golden apples?"

"What do you mean?"

"There's tons of stories with golden apples. There was a tree with golden apples in the Garden of the Hesperides that was supposed to grant immortality. Eris, the goddess of strife and discord, used a golden apple to set the Trojan War in motion. And Aphrodite gave Hippomenes a bunch of golden apples to beat Atalanta in a footrace so he could marry her."

"*Hmmm*. That didn't turn out so good."

"Exactly! It makes me regret eating one back at camp," said Maia.

"You ate a golden apple?" asked Io.

"Yes. I took it from the tree growing on the outskirts of camp."

Io frowned. "There was no such tree."

"Sure there was. Nate told me to meet Atalanta there, and I did. And I ate an apple. What's wrong?"

"The Amazons would have known of such a tree. You say golden apples are common, but the opposite is true," said Io. "You should not have eaten the apple."

"Well, I know that now. I shouldn't have done anything that Atalanta wanted me to do. *Ugh!* Do you think she planted the tree? Am I going to get sick?"

"You would have taken ill by now," said Io.

"Don't look so worried, firecracker. If there was something wrong with that apple, I'm sure a healer will be able to tell us when we meet up with the Amazons," said Nate. "But anyway, look at you, spouting all of those stories. You said you used to get all confused in Olympia."

"Yeah, you're right. I remember a lot of stories now. Could eating the golden apple have caused that?"

"I think it's more likely what's going on up there," said Nate, pointing at a particularly wide crack in the sky. "Icarus said Olympia is dying, but I think what he meant is that the barrier is failing."

Maia thought the sky was starting to look like the Grand Canyon had been flipped over and hoisted up to the heavens.

"Well, I guess everybody who wanted the worlds rejoined is going to get their wish," said Maia.

"Unless we stop Circe," said Nate, "which we will."

Maia appreciated his confidence. "When I first came here, Akantha's father, King Alphaios, had me speak before a council first assembled by Zeus to try to convince them to advise the god of thunder to take down the barrier. I was told that a war was brewing between the gods over the fate of Olympia."

"There was a war," said Augeas. "For countless days and nights, the gods battled on Mount Olympus. And in the end, there were none left to change the status of our world."

"How many gods are left?" asked Maia. "We know that Triton still rules over the seas."

"Triton was wise not to get involved," said Augeas. "Pan, god of the wild, was known to survive. Some say Aphrodite lives, but she was so disfigured that she hides in a cave not far from the entrance to the Underworld."

"Now, you want to talk about crazy, the way Aphrodite was born is the pinnacle of lunacy. She came out of sea foam that was created after Cronus took a scythe and cut off Uranus's—"

"Captain, look!" interrupted Augeas.

Flying toward them with Icarus leading were three winged horses. Icarus touched down in front of Maia and the others, and the horses followed.

"Is that Pierinos?" asked Maia, walking toward a majestic ivory stallion with a brown crescent-shaped mark on its nose.

"You've been acquainted?" asked Nate.

"Pierinos saved my life one of the first times I was brought here," said Maia, nuzzling Pierinos behind his ear.

"I believe I was instrumental in your rescue as well," said Icarus.

"It was your fault I needed to be rescued, so let's call it a draw."

Icarus turned a deep shade of red. "Yes, well, perhaps we should speed up your arrival in Varkiza."

"You mean we get to ride them? That's pretty sweet!" said Nate. "Io and Augeas can take those two, and... Maia, how about I ride on Pierinos with you?"

"Sure," said Maia as she climbed onto the horse's back. She brushed Pierinos's ivory mane with the tips of her fingers. "You ready for one more?"

Pierinos whinnied as Nate took his place behind Maia.

"If you are too heavy, perhaps I can carry Maia," said Icarus, making little effort to conceal his displeasure at the seating arrangement on Pierinos.

"Nah, I think we're good," said Nate, raising his eyebrows. "You gonna lead the way?"

"Yes, I shall," said Icarus. He pushed his shoulders back and spread his wings. Icarus's feet touched off the ground as the current of air generated by the flapping of his feathered limbs blew Maia's hair in her eyes.

"*Heeya!*" cried Maia, and Pierinos took flight followed by the other horses. Icarus flew in a circle around them and took up next to Pierinos.

"This is amazing!" yelled Nate. "What my sister wouldn't give to be riding a pegasus."

"*Hmmm.* It is a common misconception that all winged horses are named for Pegasus, the majestic steed ridden by the hero Perseus on his many adventures," said Icarus. "But the general term for a winged horse is pterippus, or pterippi for plural, stemming from the words *pteros* and *hippos.*"

"Call them what you want," said Nate, "but they're truly—"

"Wondrous," interjected Icarus, grinning back at Maia.

"When do we get to hear about your wings?" asked Maia.

Icarus rolled over in the air, spreading his wings fully. "They are a wedding gift from my wife. Or I should say the ring was the gift. When I transfer it from my left hand to my right, I gain wings."

"And they're melt-proof?"

"*Ha!* There is no wax to melt. I only need to avoid flying too close to the sun so as not to get sunburned."

"How many times have you actually fallen into the sea?"

"I lost count a long time ago," said Icarus, gliding between the three pterippi.

"And why is that?" asked Nate. "Why do certain acts happen over and over?"

"It was the will of Lord Zeus. He did not wish for the denizens of Olympia to ever lose their faith. He had to keep the wonder alive, so to speak."

"You were his playthings," said Nate.

"It is more complicated than that," said Icarus.

"You're defending him?" asked Maia. "After all the pain he caused?"

"It is not to his defense I rise, but there are subtleties that are more obvious to me now than in the past. In ancient times, before Lord Zeus abandoned the homeworld and created Olympia, there was a naturalistic relationship between gods and mortals. The gods of Olympus were born of man's desire to understand the universe. In turn, the gods watched over and tended to humanity."

"That's a very generous description of how the gods behaved," said Nate

"While Lord Zeus sought to ensure his own survival, he also sought to save those who worshipped him," said Icarus.

"Because the gods couldn't survive without their followers," said Maia.

"Yes, but also because he did not believe their followers could survive without the gods. When Lord Zeus and his brethren left the homeworld, they fully expected it to descend into chaos."

"I don't buy it," said Nate. "It was a purely selfish act. And humanity did just fine without being watched over by the gods."

"Is that so? Your world is overrun by the very evils once contained in Pandora's jar. There is perpetual war and strife. Hate washes over the homeworld in every form. Lord Zeus sought another way to further mankind. Just as he knew not to take over all the realms after the Titanomachy, sharing them instead with Poseidon and Hades and other gods as well, he knew that he could not be a dictator over Olympia. He created a council of men—"

"That was his first mistake – just having men," interrupted Maia.

"As I was saying, he created a council to allow man to advise him so as to avoid the mistakes of the past."

"I sense a 'but' coming," said Maia.

Icarus did a somersault. "You are quite right. For in the end, Lord Zeus failed. They say it took the combined might of Athena, goddess of wisdom, and Ares, god of war, to kill Lord Zeus. I doubt the effort required was that great in the end. The conflict between the gods cost Lord Zeus enormously, just as the loss of faith he experienced after word spread of Maia's existence had already weakened him."

"And what became of Athena and Ares after they killed their father?" asked Nate.

"They turned on each other. There was no rhyme or reason to the war of the gods. In the end, the matter of rejoining Olympia and the homeworld meant far less than determining who would take possession of the throne of Lord Zeus."

"And now it belongs to Circe."

"For the time being," said Icarus.

"Captain!" called Augeas as they crested a green rolling hill.

"I see it," answered Nate.

Icarus glided forward, and Maia saw where Nate was looking. In the harbor of Varkiza was moored the *Argo*. She counted at least fifty oars. The *Argo* had a long, slender hull, a shallow draft, and low clearance between the railing and the water. The square sails were massive, but paled in comparison to the prow ram. It looked powerful enough to crush a mountain.

"Beautiful, isn't she?" asked Nate, resting his chin on Maia's shoulder.

"Definitely a ship that could have taken your father across the world to find the Golden Fleece," answered Maia.

The pterippi landed not far from the dock. Maia bounded off Pierinos and hurried toward the *Argo*.

"Maia!" called her mother from behind her.

Maia skidded to a stop. She'd nearly ran past her parents.

"Mom! Dad!" she cried, "You're alright!"

"Thank Gaia, you're safe," said Matthias, embracing Maia and her mother. "Icarus told us of your encounter with Akantha. Are you injured?"

"I'm fine," answered Maia. "I was just so scared something had happened to you. Atalanta separated us after the shroud fell."

"And she paid the price for her betrayal, I understand," said Matthias. "Did Akantha say anything about Jordi?"

Maia squeezed her mother's hand. "Nothing more than a taunt, but it gave me reason to believe that he's unharmed."

Eleanor laid her head on Matthias's shoulder and sobbed. He turned and faced her. Matthias lifted his wife's chin and wiped away her tears. He pressed his lips on her forehead and managed a weak smile.

"Before this day is through, we'll have Jordi back," said Matthias. "I promise you."

Eleanor took Matthias's hand. "I'm going to keep you to that."

Only then did Maia notice what her mother was wearing – Amazonian armor. Eleanor smiled as she watched her daughter's face distort.

"The queen thought it was a good idea. She had to take it off one of your fallen sisters."

"It looks good on you," said Maia.

"Do you really think so? It came with this, too," said Eleanor, pulling a sword from her side. "Maybe you can show me how to use it."

A glint of sunlight reflected off the sword.

"Okay, but you can't stop me after five minutes and say, 'Oh, forget it,' like when I try to show you how to use the computer."

"This I cannot wait to see," said Matthias.

CHAPTER EIGHTEEN

MEASURELESS OCEANS OF SPACE

IT HAD GOTTEN QUITE CROWDED and, as a result, uncomfortably warm below deck. In addition to Maia and her parents, the *Argo* housed Icarus and Daedalus, Queen Hippolyta and Captain Penelopeia, and Nate. Conspicuously missing was Dorian. Matthias said Dorian hadn't been seen since before the attack on the camp.

"It is not wise to linger here much longer," said Daedalus. "If you desire to continue with your suicidal plans, then I will take my leave."

"Where will you go?" asked Matthias. "You yourself acknowledged that Circe has dominion over all of Olympia."

"Yes, which is why I also advised you to abandon any hope of saving this place. We must go to the homeworld before the sky fully ruptures and all of Olympia descends into primordial fire."

"We cannot know what will happen if the barrier falls," said Matthias.

"And I do not intend to find out. If you choose to stay, then I will go to the homeworld myself."

"Coward!" yelled Captain Penelopeia. "You would flee like a mouse after everything you did to create this predicament."

"I am not responsible for this!"

"You have been orchestrating matters behind the scenes for countless years," continued Captain Penelopeia. "The barrier would never have been breached if not for you."

"I merely did as Lord Zeus asked," spat Daedalus.

"You did as Zeus asked. Just as you did when King Minos asked you to create the labyrinth that held the Minotaur. And just as you did as when King Cocalus asked you to solve a riddle that ultimately led to King Minos's death."

"What is your point?"

"I already stated my point. You are a coward, leaving death and turmoil in your wake every time you run away with your tail between your legs," said Captain Penelopeia.

Daedalus jumped to his feet. "I will abide by this no longer. Stay if you so desire, but I know when to abandon a sinking ship. Come, Icarus!"

Icarus had his eyes on the floor during the entire exchange. He looked up, catching Maia's eye in the process. He smiled.

"I will not go with you."

"What? Yes, you will. Do you not remember what happens when you do not heed your father's advice?"

"I will not leave my wife," said Icarus. "Nor will I abandon my friends when there is as much at stake as the safety of a child. Go to the homeworld. I am certain you will find another powerful man to serve."

Daedalus looked as though he would explode. But the color emptied from his face as the full meaning of his son's words came to him. He cocked his head and strained to point at his son. Without a word, he stormed out of the room and ascended the ladder to the deck.

Icarus threaded his hands together over his head and stretched his palms up. "He will not be going anywhere. I threw his remaining pieces of Pandora's jar into the sea. My wife will keep them safe."

"Thank you for taking out the trash," said Maia, doing her absolute best to not burst out laughing. "But we still don't know how we're getting to Mount Olympus."

"How far is it from here?" asked Eleanor.

"It isn't a matter of distance, my love," answered Matthias. "Mount Olympus doesn't exist on the physical plane of Olympia. We need a special method of transportation."

Eleanor patted her husband's hand. "I'm going to pretend to understand what that means."

Maia chuckled. Despite her unimaginable pain, her mother retained her wit. And in his wife's presence, her father was the same pillar of strength he'd been since returning to her life.

"We must await Dorian's return," said Queen Hippolyta. "Until then, the Amazons will guard the city and the *Argo* from whatever beasts Circe intends to throw at us."

The queen stood, and the men at the table followed.

"Your courtesy flatters me, but please retain your seats," said the queen. As she crossed the room, she stopped as her eyes fell upon a shield hanging behind Nate's chair. "Is that the *aegis*? How did you come to acquire the most prized possession of the goddess of wisdom?"

Maia studied the large shield brimming with gold. In the center, in contrast to the gilded decorative edges, was an astonishingly hideous face with a protruding tongue, chipped tusks, and eyeballs that seemed to follow her. Snakes twisted around the face, adding to its repellence.

"My men recovered it from the island of Crete," said Nate. "They watched it fall from the sky, wrenched from Athena's grip during her last battle with Ares, I'd imagine."

"Quite remarkable," said Queen Hippolyta.

"Would you like it?" asked Nate.

"That is most gracious, captain," said the queen solemnly, "but the *Argo* is an apt resting place for it."

Queen Hippolyta left the room, followed by Captain Penelopeia. A moment later, Icarus stood.

"I will ask my wife if she knows of Dorian's whereabouts."

"Say, I just realized. Isn't Dorian your wife's grandfather? Doesn't that make you and Dorian family?" asked Nate.

"In a manner of speaking, are we not all relatives?" asked Icarus, winking at Maia.

Nate watched Icarus leave and then cocked his head at Maia. "What was that supposed to mean?"

"It's something he said when we first met. He has a point, though. Your father was descended from the gods. My father is, well, was a god."

"A Titan," corrected Matthias. "But your point is valid."

"So, we're related?" asked Nate, the look of distaste poorly disguised on his face.

"Only very distantly. You are the great-great-grandson of my nephew's son," said Matthias. "You and Maia are barely cousins."

"I'm sorry I asked."

* * *

MAIA STOOD ON THE PORT SIDE of the *Argo*, watching the unsettling sky. It was nearly as much red as it was blue. They were running out of time. As much as she didn't want to admit it, Maia knew they were no closer to finding Jordi than they were when they first crossed the barrier to Olympia. She hadn't completely understood what her father meant by Mount Olympus not being on the same "physical plane," but she'd kept quiet. She'd traveled to the Garden of the Hesperides through a tunnel of water created by Triton. Heracles hadn't been able to find a way there without the sea god's assistance. It must be the same with Mount Olympus, which was why Maia was increasingly worried about Dorian. He'd been gone for an entire day.

A few feet away, a member of Nate's crew who'd introduced himself as Orpheus played a lyre. The instrument's gentle notes floated across the ship. Maia found herself tapping her foot. She watched Orpheus strum the fingers of the lyre with a plectrum of carved animal bone.

"Do you mind if I join you?" asked Eleanor, stepping next to Maia. Side by side, they listened to Orpheus, the sound of the lyre intertwined with his voice, creating a low woeful sound.

"I wonder if there are any mermaids down there," Eleanor said after a moment.

"They call them sirens."

"I thought sirens were part bird."

"Those are harpies. No, maybe you're right. It's impossible to keep track."

"No worries. It'd probably freak me out if I did see a mermaid or siren, and I'm pretty much on edge already."

Maia pulled her mother into a hug. "I don't know how you're doing it, Mom."

"Doing what? Making stupid jokes? Your grandfather used to say that there wasn't a situation he'd been in yet that couldn't benefit from a dose of humor."

"I miss Grandpa," said Maia.

"I do, too. He would've thought this was all nuts."

"He'd be right."

The floorboards creaked behind them.

"I beg your pardon, Lady Eleanor, but I have something that belongs to Maia," said Captain Penelopeia, holding out a sword. "One of our sisters found it while leaving camp."

"Thank you!" said Maia, taking her beloved sword.

"The pleasure is all mine, adéxios," said Captain Penelopeia before bowing to Eleanor. Maia thought she heard a snicker as the captain walked down the gangplank.

"Adéxios?" repeated Eleanor, her eyebrows raised.

"A term of affection," said Maia, her lips pulled back in a straight line. She balanced the sword in her hand. Maia longed to use it in combat against Akantha.

"They're quite impressive," said Eleanor, pointing to a group of Amazons patrolling the pier.

"You'd fit right in, Mom."

"*Ha!* Thank you, but no."

"I mean it," said Maia. "You're just as tough as any of them – even Queen Hippolyta. It doesn't matter what life throws at you."

"What's the alternative? When your father disappeared, I still had to take care of you. And when Grandma got sick or when Grandpa got hurt at work, I couldn't give up. And I won't give up now either. I'm completely out of my element, and I can't pretend to understand half of what's going on. But I trust your father. And I trust you. Everything is going to be okay."

"You're incredible, you know that?"

"I'd have to be to have a daughter like you," said Eleanor, caressing Maia's hair. "Now that we both have swords, how about you teach me a thing or two?"

"You're on!"

* * *

THE AFTERNOON WORE ON INTO EVENING. Sitting in a plaza near the pier, Maia nursed a bruise on her cheek. Her mother had some unexpected skill with a sword.

The plaza was all but empty. A woman in threadbare robes stood behind a hodgepodge of baskets filled with fruits and breads. A cat circled her feet, rubbing against her legs. The woman shooed the animal, but it returned straightaway.

Kra-kow!

A streak of red lightning tore across the sky. It was fractured far worse than just a few hours ago. A horse reared back, pulling a young boy to the ground. Maia crossed the plaza to offer her assistance.

"*Whoa! Whoa!* Easy fella," said Maia, grabbing the reins. The horse snorted and tossed its head back and forth, but calmed after a few seconds. "Here you go."

The boy took the reins from Maia. "Thank you! I thought he was going to run away. My father would be furious."

"Not a problem," said Maia, petting the horse's nose.

"You are an Amazon," said the boy in a low squeal.

"Yes, my name is Maia. What's yours?"

"I am Orion."

"Are you a hunter?" asked Maia, squinting.

"No, I am a farmer, like my father and his father before him. My mother liked the story of Orion. It was one of her favorites."

Maia sensed grief in Orion's voice. "Did something happen to your mother?"

Orion's bottom lip quivered, and soon tears rolled down his cheeks. "I woke up one morning, and she was missing. My father said she had gone to fetch water, but she never returned. She is not the only person to disappear. More than half of the town has vanished. My father does not think I heard him talking to my uncle, but they say it is Circe the witch. She takes people and – *sniff!* – changes them into hideous monsters."

Maia dropped to one knee in front of Orion and took his hands. The boy whimpered and looked up at her. Maia pulled him into her arms.

"I'm so sorry, Orion. I wish I could tell you I know what happened to your mother," said Maia, "but I know wherever she is, she's thinking about you and keeping you in her heart. Can you do that, too?"

Orion nodded his head. Maia spotted a man walking toward them. He put his hand on Orion's arm, and the boy spun around, clutching his leg.

"I hope my son was not bothering you," said Orion's father.

"Not at all. He's a very brave young man," said Maia.

Beneath his tear-filled eyes, Orion gave Maia a shaky smile.

"Come," said Orion's father, taking the horse's reins in one hand and his son's hand in the other. Orion waved goodbye to Maia as they crossed the plaza.

The crunching of footsteps on the gritty cobblestones signaled that someone was approaching her from behind. Maia put her hand on the hilt of her sword.

"He seemed like a sweet kid," said Nate, bumping Maia's shoulder with his own.

Maia took her hand off her sword. "Were you watching us?"

"I was coming to find you," said Nate. "Icarus got a message from Dorian. He'll be here soon."

"Finally!" exclaimed Maia as she watched Orion and his father exit the plaza. "We need to put an end to all of this. That little boy thinks Circe abducted his mother, and she probably did. He's just an ordinary kid living in an extraordinary place that's about to be destroyed. What's going to happen to him? And all the other

people that Zeus trapped here so that he and the gods could survive?"

"I don't know," answered Nate, "but Dorian will have some
answers. We're going to get through this. And we'll save as many
people as we can."

Maia looked to the sun hanging over the mountains.

"*Surrounded, detached, in measureless oceans of space.*"

"What'd you say?" asked Nate.

"It's from a poem that I didn't understand until now."

"And why is that?"

"For a long time, I thought I was alone, trying but failing to
connect with other people. Or so I thought," said Maia. "But now I
know I'm not alone. And that's why we're going to win."

CHAPTER NINETEEN

BREACHING THE GATE

CLOUDS LOOMED OVERHEAD, but Maia scarcely noticed them. Her attention was drawn to her right hand, which Nate had taken in his left hand as they hurried to the pier.

"You're holding my hand," said Maia.

"You're very perceptive," countered Nate.

"And why are you holding my hand?"

"Well, jeez, Miss Maia, I don't know how to say this, but I've got an awful crush on you, and I was hoping I could take you to the prom."

"You're hysterical," said Maia, tugging her hand away.

Nate scooped it up again.

"I wish I could have," said Nate.

"What?"

"Taken you to the prom."

"You're completely mental, you know that?"

"Did you go to your prom?"

"No."

"You didn't? Why not?"

"I didn't feel like it. Jackie didn't want to go because 'Block' lives in Spain, so the two of us went to the movies. Did you go to your prom?"

"Yep! And I was voted 'Prom King' and everything."

"Really?"

"Nope. We'd gotten word a few days before that my dad had been killed," said Nate, giving Maia's hand a squeeze. "I didn't feel much like dancing after that."

"That must've been awful."

"Well, truth be told, I didn't feel much like going in the first place. Tuxedos make me itch."

"I meant about your—"

"I know what you meant, silly. It was a rough time, but made even rougher by all of the secrets that came flooding out after he died. My sister didn't know any of it. I think she was too sad to be angry about it at the time, but now she's just angry – at my mother, at me, and I guess at my father, too."

"Has she been to Olympia?" asked Maia.

"Julia? Nah, she's got no interest. At least that's what she says now. I offered to bring her here when I was going back and forth, but she turned me down. I haven't been home since I came here after Christmas."

"Isn't your mother worried?"

"My mom's a soldier. She understands why I'm here," said Nate. "She's been on a special assignment for months. I'm not even sure where she and Julia are stationed. That's why your letters came back."

"By the way, you're still holding my hand."

"I know."

* * *

A CROWD BLOCKED THEIR WAY as Maia and Nate neared the pier. The reason for all the attention was made apparent very quickly. Next to the *Argo* loomed Triton, at least twenty-five feet tall. The setting sun caused his beard to glisten. The sea god's expression was amusing. Maia thought it bordered between contempt and disdain.

"That's a big pitchfork."

"It's called a trident," said Maia, smacking Nate across the chest.

Nate was correct, though. The sea god's trident was as large as he. Triton twisted his weapon to the right and then back again to the left. Maia noticed that the sky reacted to the trident's movement, funnels of clouds forming then dissipating.

Pushing their way through the crowd, Maia and Nate joined her parents and Dorian at the end of the pier. The trio looked as irritated as the sea god.

"What's wrong?" asked Maia, putting her arm around her mother's shoulders.

"We're waiting for Daedalus," answered Matthias.

"Why?"

"Because we need to make a human sacrifice before we can journey to Mount Olympus, and everyone agreed he was the most expendable," said Dorian.

Maia swallowed a laugh. "That was good. You almost had me for a second."

"CAN WE GET ON WITH THIS?" boomed Triton. The pier swayed as he lifted the fins of his massive green tail from the water, only to splash them down again. Maia and the others were doused with seawater.

"Your son has a temper," said Nate between coughs. "Are we really waiting for Daedalus?"

"Whether he realizes it or not, he may hold the key to defeating Circe," answered Dorian.

Above them came the sound of wings flapping over the protestations of a red-faced Daedalus. His son Icarus darted down and dropped Daedalus on the pier. He rolled on the wooden planks and came to a stop at Maia's feet. Icarus flew up again and turned in the air before diving down onto an outbreak of rocks. There was a considerable splash of water, from which came a beautiful young woman with a tail as green as Triton's. Maia felt her face go red as Icarus planted a firm kiss on the woman's lips.

"This is outrageous!" yelled Daedalus as he pulled himself to his feet. "I told you I wanted nothing to do with this suicide mission."

"You'll play your part, willingly or not," said Matthias. "Now climb aboard!"

Captain Penelopeia appeared from behind them and stabbed at Daedalus with a spear.

"That is quite enough!" yelled Daedalus as he maneuvered to dodge the point of the spear. "I will board the wretched vessel."

Captain Penelopeia jabbed Daedalus in the backside as he stomped up the gangplank, causing the old man to sound like a pig chased around a farmyard. Nate held up his hand to give Captain Penelopeia a high five.

"I think it is a fine ship," said Captain Penelopeia, awkwardly slapping Nate's hand.

"Thank you!" said Nate.

"Have you figured out how we're going to get to Mount Olympus?" asked Maia.

"On Nate's 'fine ship,' of course," answered Dorian.

"Wait, what now?" asked Nate. "How are we supposed to sail our way up a mountain, figuratively or not?"

"This ship has done far more wondrous feats than merely reaching the top of a mountain, even one on another place of existence," said Dorian. "You need to study your father's exploits at greater length. Still, we require assistance especially given our need for haste. My son is prepared to help."

"When do we leave?" asked Maia.

"We were just waiting for you," said Matthias, "and for you as well, Captain Nathanial. The *Argo* is your ship."

"Are my men aboard?"

"Yes, those who are not patrolling the city, as well as Queen Hippolyta and several of her sisters," said Dorian. "We must leave right away."

"Hang on a second," said Nate. "The *Argo* isn't ready to go. We have to lower the sails and get those oars in the water. That's going to take some—"

"We need the sails raised and the oars are fine as they are. Trust me, captain. There is nothing more to arrange."

Eleanor squeezed Maia's hand. "Be careful."

"You're not coming with us?" asked Maia.

"I don't think I'll be of much help on Mount Olympus," said Eleanor, brushing Maia's hair from her face.

"But—"

"Your mother will be safer here. Captain Penelopeia leads the effort to secure the city. Triton will remain as well."

"Mom, I... I love you so much," said Maia, burying her face in her mother's chest. "We'll bring Jordi back, I promise."

Maia felt her mother's arms wrap around her, joined moments later by her father's. Warm in their embrace, Maia silently prayed that her brother would be safe in their protection before long.

Stepping back, Maia took her mother's hands. "You really do look good in armor."

Eleanor chuckled. "Not as good as you. It suits you."

Maia let go of her mother's hands. Her father held her mother's chin.

"Eleanor, I will—"

"Shut up and kiss me."

"As you wish."

Maia glanced over at Nate, who was doing his best not to look back. Their eyes met, and Nate gave her a warm smile showing a row of white teeth. Maia's heart seemed to give an extra beat.

"Come, Maia," said Matthias, reaching out his hand.

With a final glance at her mother and Captain Penelopeia, Maia trailed her father up the gangplank, followed by Dorian and Nate. As Maia stepped on board the *Argo*, Icarus touched down a few feet ahead of her.

"I take it that was your wife you were kissing?" asked Maia.

"Yes," said Icarus. "I would have introduced you to her, but—"

"Nope," said Maia, waving her hand. "I'm sure I'll meet her another time. By the way, your father is pretty pissed."

Icarus looked over his shoulder at his father. The great artificer was sitting on a pile of ropes rubbing his bottom.

"He doesn't subscribe to many different feelings," said Icarus, moving his ring from one hand to the next. The wings protruding from his back shook and shrank away. A single feather wafted to the floor.

"Can I try that thing?" asked Maia, her eyes studying the ring.

"Maia! Come here, please," called Matthias.

"Just give me a second," said Maia to Icarus before rushing over to her father. She wondered what color wings she'd sprout if she put on the ring.

"You should sit," said Matthias.

Maia took an accounting of the crew. In addition to Dorian, Icarus, Daedalus, her father, and herself, the *Argo* housed Nate and seven Argonauts – Orpheus, Augeas, Menoetius, Poeas, Hylas, Zetes, and Tydeus – as well as Queen Hippolyta and six Amazons –

Io, Sinope, Priene, Cyme, Lampedo, and Thyra. Maia hoped they were enough to battle Circe and her army of horrors.

The entire ship shuddered. A spray of seawater came over the bow. Clouds formed above the boat, only to part a moment later. With a great wrenching sound, the *Argo* began to move. But the movement wasn't forward or backward. Or even side to side. The *Argo* was rising up in the air.

"You really should sit," said Matthias, patting the wooden bench next to him.

The *Argo* rose higher and higher, somewhat unsteadily at first and then more smoothly. Maia sat next to her father as the ship broke through a layer of clouds.

"This is new," said Maia.

"Triton has it all under control," said Matthias.

"So, how is this working?" asked Maia. "Is Triton going to—"

"Wait and see," interrupted Matthias.

An icy wind blew across the deck of the ship. Trembling, Maia watched her breath freeze before her. She rubbed her arms, her bare skin rough and spiky. The *Argo* emerged from another cloudbank, and the chill was gone. Maia gasped. There wasn't anything before them except for a sparse number of stars.

"You can stand up now," said Matthias. "It should be smooth sailing for the moment."

Maia put her hands behind her and pushed off the bench. Standing, she tapped the deck of the ship with the tip of her right foot.

"Don't worry, Maia," said Matthias. "It is perfectly safe."

"Are we in outer space?"

"Not exactly. We are between worlds. Triton used his trident to create a waterspout to propel us into the space that separates the land and the sky."

"It's beautiful," said Maia.

More and more stars appeared around them. The *Argo* sailed forward. Maia was reminded of a hot air balloon ride she'd taken with Jackie at a state fair. She caught Nate's eye at the wheel of the ship. He shrugged his shoulders. Maia thought he must be as surprised as she. She traced the outline of the prow ram against the star-filled sky. Maia turned her head sideways as a glint of color appeared before the prow ram. There was a sudden noiseless explosion of light, and the *Argo* was surrounded by iridescent colors of the rainbow.

"We're nearly at the gates of Mount Olympus. These colors," said Matthias, waving his hand, "are all that remain of the goddess Iris. She was the messenger of the gods before Hermes. Her wings were so striking they were capable of bringing light to even the darkest corners of the Underworld. But, like so many others, Iris fell to the chaos wrought by the war of the gods."

The colors faded as the ship sped up. Nate jumped down from the helm and made his way next to Maia.

"I don't know what I was even doing up there. It's not like I was steering or anything."

"Well, you did look impressive," said Maia, looking at her feet to hide her face.

"Laugh it up, smirky," said Nate, grazing Maia's side with his elbow. "We seem to be going faster. Does anyone have an idea what comes next?"

Dorian and Icarus joined them. Maia glanced at Daedalus. The "mighty" artificer hadn't moved since boarding.

"My son's waterspout is gaining in strength," said Dorian. "We must brace ourselves."

"What's happening?" asked Maia, but there was no need for anyone to answer.

The last of Iris's colors dissipated as a massive bronze gateway adorned with bolts of lightning materialized before them. The *Argo* was headed straight for it. There was a lurch as if a hand had pushed the ship forward at the last moment.

"We're going to—"

CRASH!

The gates burst open as the *Argo* struck them at full speed. There was a booming cracking sound, which reminded Maia of the tree that had fallen across the street in front of her house during a hurricane last summer. The prow ram of the *Argo* splintered apart and fell backward, crushing the forecastle deck of the ship. The right gate broke free from its invisible hinge and struck the *Argo's* stern, causing the ship to turn.

"Brace yourselves!" yelled Nate as he clung to the mast.

The *Argo* rolled forward and slammed against the slope of a mountain. Maia fell to the deck alongside her father. The ship shuddered, sliding several yards before coming to rest on an embankment.

Maia pushed herself off the deck and crawled to her father's side. A few feet away a hatch burst open and from it emerged Queen Hippolyta. The queen straightened her crown.

"So, shall we get on with it?"

CHAPTER TWENTY

THE CLIMB

THE *ARGO'S* ILL-FATED PASSENGERS assembled on what remained of the deck. Nate surveyed the damage to the forecastle. The prow ram was just as majestic in ruin as it was in its former place at the bow of the ship.

"Are you okay?" asked Maia.

"Yeah, I'm fine," said Nate, his voice hollow. "I guess it was the only way we were going to get through the gates. The prow ram was made of timber from Zeus's sacred grove of oak trees in Dodona. It could withstand almost anything."

"We're actually on Mount Olympus."

"Looks that way, firecracker."

CREEEEAAAAAK!

The *Argo* shifted, and Nate grabbed Maia's wrist.

"We have to get off the ship," said Nate.

Maia nodded her head in agreement.

"Everyone, this way!" yelled Nate, pointing to a gap in the side of the ship. Maia caught her father's eye, and he directed her with his hand to follow Nate. She slid through the gap, followed by her father, Dorian, and Daedalus. Icarus landed next to them, wings jutting from his back. All around them, Argonauts and Amazons jumped ship.

CREEEEAAAAAK!

"I suggest we keep moving," said Queen Hippolyta.

"Agreed," said Dorian. "Follow me."

The rag-tag group followed Dorian away from the *Argo*. They came to the edge of the embankment.

"Now what?" asked Maia.

"We need the *Argo* to get back home," said Nate.

"You and your men stay and see what repairs to your ship you can manage," said Dorian. "The rest of us will make our way to the summit."

"And how do you propose we do that?" asked Daedalus.

"We have to climb past that ridge," answered Dorian, pointing to a rocky outcrop several yards above them. "There should be a staircase."

"I'm coming with you," said Nate. "I honestly don't know how much good I'll do here."

"Thyra is a most capable carpenter," said Queen Hippolyta. "She will assist in the repairs."

"Orpheus should come with us as well," said Dorian. "We may require his talents."

"Augeas, I leave you in charge," said Nate. "See what you can do to put her back together."

"Yes, captain," said Augeas.

Queen Hippolyta and the Amazons leapt into action, scaling the side of the mountain.

"Or perhaps we can fly. Please, allow me," said Icarus, reaching out a hand to Maia.

"I can manage, thank you."

"Suit yourself. Father?"

Daedalus shook his head, but after a moment he raised up his arms so Icarus could hoist him. Icarus kicked off the ground and flew past the Amazons and Orpheus, disappearing through a cloud. He returned a moment later.

"That was quick," said Maia.

"It is more wondrous than I could ever have imagined," said Icarus when he landed.

"What'd you see up there?" asked Nate.

"The realm of the gods," answered Icarus, "or at least what is left of it."

* * *

MAIA WAITED FOR ICARUS to make his last unexpected delivery. Orpheus had lost his grip and slid down the side of the mountain. Icarus landed next to Dorian, laying Orpheus on the ground.

"Is everyone here?" asked Icarus.

Maia looked around. The Amazons, with Queen Hippolyta in the lead, had gotten to the summit first. Io was kneeling over Orpheus. The musician had a large gash on the side of his head.

"Sit still," said Io, as she wrapped Orpheus's head with a make-shift bandage.

"I am afraid that I am not much of a climber," said Orpheus. "These hands are better suited for playing the lyre."

"Nonsense," said Io with a flicker of a smile.

Maia raised her eyebrows, catching the Amazon's attention. Her grin quickly changed to pursed lips.

"There. That will stop the bleeding," said Io before marching over to Queen Hippolyta.

"Battles make for strange bedfellows," said Dorian.

"I suppose," said Maia, glancing at Nate. He was standing with her father, and whatever he was saying was enough to bring a smile to Matthias's face. "Do you think Yaya and Apolyn are okay?"

The question seemed to catch Dorian by surprise. "Oh, I am sure they are well. I would trust Apolyn with my life."

"And your heart?" asked Maia.

"As I said... strange bedfellows."

"Why? Because he's a guy?"

"No, Maia, I am quite comfortable sharing my heart with a man as I am with a woman. But when I brought Apolyn to the home-world from Olympia, I did not intend to fall in love with him. It was imprudent given the state of both worlds."

"Love is love," said Maia.

"Yes, thank you for that pearl of wisdom. My point is that I worry what will happen to Apolyn when this conflict is over."

"If it actually ever does end. What's our next step?"

"Funny you should put it that way," said Dorian.

The mists shifted and a stairway carved into the side of the mountain became visible.

"How long a climb is it?"

"I honestly do not know. I never had to take the stairs before I gave up godhood."

Maia stood at the first step. Her father appeared by her side and placed a hand on her shoulder.

"Do you think Circe is up there?" asked Maia.

"If she is then we must exercise caution. I believe we lost the element of surprise when we crash landed. Queen Hippolyta will take the lead with the Amazons."

"I'm an Amazon."

"Yes, but you will stay with your uncle and me."

"But—"

"For our protection, not yours. Nate will follow with Orpheus. Icarus will scout ahead."

"What about Daedalus? I still don't understand why we brought him."

"I don't either," said Matthias, "but we must play every card we have."

"Including the joker."

* * *

THERE WERE A STAGGERING NUMBER of steps. Several times, after turning a corner, Maia thought they'd made some progress toward reaching the end, but more stairs appeared. Icarus flew up ahead and promised to report back when the end was near, but so far he'd only shared in Maia's frustration.

"This is pointless," spat Daedalus. "We are mortals. We will never reach the top. And even if we do, we are certain to meet with death. Hades will be welcoming us all to the Underworld before the sun sets."

"Keep it up, and you'll be the first one on his doorstep," said Nate.

"Quiet!" cried Io from the lead.

Maia dropped to one knee and unsheathed her sword. Seconds ticked by.

"Sister, what is it?"

"It sounds like... LOOK OUT!"

Maia pushed up against the mountainside, pulling Dorian alongside her. A barrel came tumbling down the steps, knocking into Daedalus. He plummeted past Nate but crashed into Orpheus, both of them disappearing beneath a cloud.

"No!" called Maia, bounding down the steps. Nate grabbed her by the upper arm as Icarus swooped past them.

"Hang on, firecracker. You won't be able to see anything in the clouds. You could fall off the mountain."

"Icarus may need our help."

"Nate is right, Maia," said Matthias. "We must keep climbing."

"Hold your ground," called Queen Hippolyta. "Listen!"

An eerie melody fell upon them. It had a mournful quality, not unlike the music Orpheus played. But between the notes was an occasional burst of laughter.

"Oh, this is not good," said Dorian.

"What is it?" asked Matthias.

"It is not a what, but a who. It is my nephew Dionysus."

"The god of wine?" asked the queen.

"And ritual madness and religious ecstasy. He of all the Olympians may be taking the most delight from the chaos that has overtaken Olympia."

"Should we keep going?" asked Nate.

"We have no choice. Keep your wits about you."

They pushed forward, surprised to find themselves free from stairs for the moment. In a small field of mud and brown grass, surrounded by weedy bushes of grapes, stood a circular temple. In the middle of the structure lay Dionysus upon a bed covered with crimson red sheets.

"MORE WINE!" bellowed Dionysus. "Bring another barrel here!"

"Who's he talking to?" whispered Maia.

"Your guess is as good as mine," replied Dorian.

"I said, more wine! Who does a god of Olympus have to... Oy! You there," said Dionysus, pointing at Queen Hippolyta, "bring me more wine, wench."

Maia swallowed thickly.

Queen Hippolyta placed her hand on the hilt of her sword. "Excuse me while I take care of something."

"Your highness," said Io, stepping in front of the queen. "He is not worth it."

"No, but they may certainly be," said Queen Hippolyta, tilting her chin forward.

Maia followed the queen's line of sight. In the distance appeared a trio of birds. Two of them carried a barrel between them. As they neared, it became clear that they were no ordinary birds. They had the heads of women, long boney claws, and pale protruding stomachs. One of them cried out as it defecated in flight.

"Harpies," spat Dorian.

"To arms," cried Queen Hippolyta.

The sound of flapping wings met Maia's ears as Icarus landed beside her.

"Where are your father and Orpheus?"

"I brought them back to the *Argo*. They were in no position to continue," said Icarus, readying a bow and arrow.

The harpies carrying the barrel flew past Dionysus's temple, hurtling their cargo down the side of the mountain.

"NO!" cried Dionysus. "By Zeus, you are as cruel as you are revolting."

The trio of monsters circled back and landed atop the temple.

"*SCAW!*"

"Screech away, beasts, for your time is done. Look!" Dionysus called, pointing at Maia and her comrades. "My father has finally sent someone to end my torment."

"You are mistaken, nephew," said Dorian. "We are not interested in you or Zeus's hounds. We seek Circe."

"Nephew? You declare yourself to be a relative of Dionysus?"

"Where is Circe?" asked Matthias.

"Kill the harpies, and I will tell you anything you want," said Dionysus.

"Tell us where we can find Circe, and we may consider assisting you," said Dorian.

"*SCAW!*"

"We are wasting time," scowled Io. "Look! The stairs continue beyond the temple. Ignore the god of wine and his tormentors."

"*SCAW! SCAW! SCAW!*"

"I don't think they liked that," said Maia.

The largest of the harpies pushed off the temple, shaking its columns. The two others followed, and the columns gave way, crashing on top of Dionysus.

"*SCAW! SCAW! SCAW!*"

"Form a perimeter!" called Queen Hippolyta.

Maia and the others created a ring with Icarus in the center. He flew up and let loose a barrage of arrows, catching one of the monsters in the leg. It grabbed the arrow and pulled it free, throwing it back at Icarus as it charged forward. Io tossed her shield, slicing off the creature's head. Its body fell at Maia's feet.

"*SCAW! SCAW! SCAW!*"

"Two more!"

The remaining pair of harpies hung over the group, dropping phlegm and guano.

"Maintain formation and head toward the stairs," shouted Queen Hippolyta.

Icarus fired off more arrows, but failed to strike the harpies. The beasts soared high into the air and then flipped backward as they charged the group. Maia locked eyes with one of the creatures as it reached out its claws. She pulled back her sword and thrust it into the harpy's throat. Behind her, Queen Hippolyta did the same to the final harpy.

"Well done, Maia," said her father, putting his arm around her.

"Thanks, but that almost seemed too easy," said Maia.

"Agreed," said the queen. "Circe would have better protection this close to the summit. Let us ask the god of wine."

Dorian approached the ruins of the temple where Dionysus lie groaning.

"Where is Circe, nephew?"

"She is not here. She is—"

A spray of blood came from Dionysus's mouth, an axe protruding from his back.

At the base of the stairs stood Hephaestus, god of metalworking, holding an identical axe.

"Leave this place or you will suffer the same fate!"

CHAPTER TWENTY-ONE

SANCTUARY LOST

ICARUS TOUCHED DOWN BESIDE DORIAN. He looked back and forth between Dorian and Hephaestus.

"Take heed, Dorian. We dare not challenge a god of Olympus at his peak strength," said Icarus.

"Allow me to handle my nephew... my other nephew, that is."

"The artificer's son is wise to caution you," cried Hephaestus. "You have no dominion here, uncle."

"You know me?"

"My brother Dionysus was too far gone to recognize you, but, with or without your godhood, you smell the same – like low tide."

"And you are as unworthy as always to sit beside the children of Cronus. Let us pass."

"Over my corpse."

"So be it," said Dorian.

Maia unsheathed her sword, ready to fight at Dorian's side. She glanced at the quivering body of Dionysus and for a moment thought he'd survived the assault by Hephaestus. But the movement she'd witnessed was not exclusive to Dionysus. The broken columns of the temple shook along with the muddy pitch beneath her feet.

HAAARRRAAASH!

The clatter was deafening. And the source of it was getting closer.

HAAARRRAAASH!

At the edge of the field appeared an object similar to a worn, rusty metal garbage can. It was quickly joined by three more. Just beyond them, from the mist surrounding the mountain emerged the apex of a helmet. Steam hissed where the metal cylinders dug into the ground.

HAAARRRAAASH!

With an earth-shuddering crash, a metal giant jumped onto the field. The ground beneath its feet burned. The creature swung its head to and fro surveying Maia and her compatriots.

HAAARRRAAASH!

The giant's jaws creaked apart to create an opening twice as big as when it cried out. A spray of molten rock shot forth from its mouth.

"Stand back!" cried Queen Hippolyta, as she and the Amazons lifted their shields in tight formation. The molten rock struck their armors with fury. "Forward!"

The Amazons charged the giant. Its jaws clamped shut, steam gushing from the corners of its mouth. The giant raised its arms in a Y formation. Its fists shook as it let out another raspy cry. The giant plunged its rusty metal fingers into the ground before the Amazons could reach it, sending them tumbling backwards. They sprang to their feet and circled the giant, striking blow after blow at its fingers. The giant swatted at the Amazons as it stood upright, smashing Io on the side of her head. The Amazon struck the ground several feet away, her body smoldering and lifeless. Queen Hippolyta rushed to Io's side as the remaining Amazons mounted another assault. The queen pressed her forehead to Io's and whispered a prayer. Stabbing her sword into the ground, Queen Hippolyta rushed back into the fight.

Icarus took flight, circling the giant. He dodged the creature's fist and loaded his bow. In quick succession, he shot several arrows at the giant's eyes, but they caught fire and crumbled upon impact.

"We must disable the monster before it can replenish!" cried Dorian.

"What do you mean?" yelled Maia.

"Look at its ankle," said Matthias.

The giant stood with its right leg back. From its right ankle jutted out the head of an enormous bronze nail. Shooting up from the nail was a vein, filled up to the giant's thigh with a bubbling liquid. The giant swung its head toward Maia.

HAAARRRAAASH!

The liquid shot up further, past the giant's waist.

"If the molten rock reaches its mouth, it'll blast us again," cried Matthias. "Icarus, you must aim for the giant's ankle."

Icarus swooped down closer, hovering just overhead. "I do not know if my arrows can pierce its skin."

"What if we can pull the nail out?" asked Nate. "It's worth a shot."

"It's too much of a risk for one of us to get so close," said Matthias.

HAAARRRAAASH!

The liquid bubbled up to the center of the giant's chest.

"Whatever you are going to do, you must do it fast!" cried Queen Hippolyta, dodging a rock the giant had wrenched from the mountain.

"I can do it," said Maia. "Icarus can drop me from behind."

"That's insane," said Matthias. "I won't allow it."

"I can pry the nail out with my shield. All you have to do is distract it."

"Good plan, firecracker, but I'll be the one doing the prying," said Nate.

"No, you're not strong enough! And Dad, you stand a better chance at distracting it than I do."

Matthias put his hand on Maia's forearm. "When the nail is removed, the molten rock will spew out like a fountain. You must—"

"I'll be fine," interrupted Maia, raising her arms. "It'll be just like we practiced at the warehouse – in and out."

Icarus flapped his wings and spiraled down to grab Maia under her arms. The giant grabbed another stone and hurled it at Matthias, Dorian and Nate. They dove to the ground and quickly scrambled to their feet, pulling in close to the Amazons. The liquid reached the giant's neck. Steam escaped from its jaws as it raised its arms again in a Y formation.

"We must keep it occupied," said Matthias to Queen Hippolyta.

"And what exactly do you think we have been doing?" replied the queen.

Icarus flew past the giant and rolled back.

"Are you ready?" asked Icarus.

Maia gripped her shield in front of her with both hands. She lifted her arms slightly, allowing Icarus to maintain his grip while readying to strike.

HAAARRRAAASH!

"Shields!" cried Queen Hippolyta.

"Now!" yelled Maia.

Icarus dove at the giant's right leg as the creature wrenched open its jaws. Maia raised her arms fully over her head, slipping free from Icarus. As she was about to hit the ground, she thrust her shield forward, striking the giant at the point where the head of the nail protruded. The nail gave way, and a jet of molten rock sprayed against Maia's shield. She rolled to her side out of the path of the giant's lifeblood. It pooled at the edge of the field, obliterating the terrain as it dripped over the side.

The giant fell to its knees and collapsed to the ground, crushing the remains of Dionysus and his temple. A final spray of steam came from its mouth as it blinked its eyes. The red pupils shrank away leaving only darkness.

"No!" yelled Hephaestus from the steps. "He was my last creation. He was my... child." The god of metalworking turned and ran up the steps.

"After him!" ordered Queen Hippolyta.

Matthias ran forward, leaping over the fallen giant's leg. "Are you alright?"

"I'm fine," answered Maia, hugging her father. "We have to stop Hephaestus."

"He won't get far," said Nate, bounding past them. Icarus whooshed by overhead. By the time Maia and Matthias reached the steps, they were the last in pursuit.

As she ran up the steps, Maia felt a stabbing pain in her left calf. She'd been struck by the giant's blood, only realizing it once she'd begun running. Maia reached down and brushed away the hardening liquid. Blood dripped down her leg. Grimacing, Maia raced up the steps. She caught up to the father as he disappeared around a corner. When Maia herself rounded the corner, she skidded to a stop. Before her lay a seemingly endless field of burnt and broken columns. Massive temples were toppled over and upended. Vines twisted between the splintered marbles. Above the field amidst a sky of red swirled a massive black cloud, lightning crackling at its center. The wind howled as it wound its way through the columns.

"This can't be right," said Maia, dropping her shield. "Where's Circe?"

Dorian faced Maia. "Do not despair. If she is here, we will find her."

"If?" repeated Nate. "If she's not here, then where would she be?"

"He will give us answers," said Queen Hippolyta, throwing Hephaestus at their feet.

Dorian kneeled and grasped Hephaestus by his hair. "Hello, nephew."

Hephaestus pushed his hands against the ground, but Icarus landed on his back. Queen Hippolyta pulled her sword and swept the side of the god's face.

"You dare! I gave you that sword," spat Hephaestus. "I gave you all of those weapons, and you dare use them against me?"

"Where is Circe?" asked Dorian, pulling Hephaestus's head back.

The god of metalworking stared at Dorian, his curled back lips beginning to quiver. A guttural noise rose from his chest and Hephaestus let out a cackle. Dorian let him go, and Hephaestus proceeded to roar with laughter into the ground.

"He has gone mad," said Queen Hippolyta.

"Enough of this," said Matthias, kicking Hephaestus in the arm. "Where is Circe?"

"*Ha ha ha ha haah!* You thought you would find her here? No, that witch was sadly disappointed when she arrived. Heracles made sure of that. He left nothing standing when he marched on Olympus. Circe took a few odds and ends, but I dare say she was too late to take anything of value."

"Heracles did all of this?" asked Maia.

"He destroyed anything that was left after the war of the gods," said Hephaestus. "He took my father's lightning bolt and laid waste to it all."

"How did you survive?"

"It would take more than a little lightning to kill a son of Zeus. I did not choose sides in the war, so I was not weakened. When Heracles arrived, Athena and Ares had all but destroyed each other in their battle to assume Zeus's throne. It was easy enough for Heracles to finish them off."

"So, it was Athena and Ares?" asked Dorian, his eyes narrowed. "I wondered which of my brethren managed to vanquish the mighty Zeus."

"*Ha ha!* Does this sadden you? Does it pain you to see Olympus in ruins?" asked Hephaestus. He buried his head in the ground, muffling his laughter.

Maia felt a rush of blood to her head. Her vision blurred as Hephaestus's laughter echoed in her ears. Maia shook off the dizzy spell and turned her attention to Dorian.

"Silence nephew, or you will find yourself cast off Mount Olympus," said Dorian, brushing past Hephaestus.

"What?" cried Hephaestus, raising his head.

Queen Hippolyta and Nate each took Hephaestus by an arm and dragged him to the edge of the field.

"Are you mad? I am the god—"

"Hopefully, it will take more than a little lightning *and* a fall to earth to kill a son of Zeus," interrupted Queen Hippolyta.

"One can only hope," said Nate as he and the queen swung Hephaestus back in unison.

"You would not dare!"

"Tell us what we need to know!" shouted Dorian. "What would have remained for Circe to take?"

"Jars. She took useless jars!" spat Hephaestus. "Zeus only kept them in his temple because Hera had molded them."

Queen Hippolyta and Nate dropped Hephaestus on the ground. The god of metalworking sat on his bottom, scowling. He and Daedalus could be twins, thought Maia.

"Jars!" repeated Matthias. "Dorian, what do you remember of the day Zeus created Olympia?"

"What do you mean?"

"Zeus needed our godly energies and those of Hera, but he did not simply syphon them from us and create another world. He had to contain them before putting his plan in motion."

"I do not recall," said Dorian.

"One is able to breach the barrier between Olympia and the homeworld using fragments of Pandora's jar. What if Zeus used similar vessels to contain our energies before he could finalize his plans? Would such vessels be capable of destroying the barrier permanently?"

"But we know not if these vessels existed," said Icarus. "Perhaps Circe took the jars for another reason."

"Your father would know," said Matthias.

"Well, if there is no longer a reason to remain here, perhaps we should return to the *Argo* and ask him," said Queen Hippolyta.

"We can't just leave!" blurted Maia. "We still don't know where Circe took Jordi. How do we go back to Mom and tell her this was all for nothing?"

"Your mother will understand."

"You're so sure of that? You thought we'd find Circe here, but that turned out to be wrong. And now you want to go chasing after some jars that you only *think* may have existed? For what reason?"

"If we find the jars, then we will find Circe... and your brother," said Dorian.

"Are you freaking kidding me?" cried Maia. "You don't know that! You don't know... "

"Maia!" yelled Matthias as his daughter fell to the ground.

"Look at her leg! She's losing a lot of blood," said Nate.

"Let go... of me," mumbled Maia.

"Be still," said Matthias. "We'll bring you to the *Argo*."

Maia blinked her eyes several times before darkness settled before them.

CHAPTER TWENTY-TWO

THE MISSING JARS

THE ROOM SWAYED, and Maia sensed her stomach drop. Heaving herself up, she turned to her side and vomited. Maia felt a hand brush her hair back. Panting, she looked into her father's eyes.

"Thank goodness you're well," said Matthias.

"I, uh, just puked, but okay, I guess I'm well," said Maia, wiping her hand across her mouth. "Can someone get me—"

"Here," said Nate, handing her a wet cloth. "Your father's right, though. You had us all worried."

"What happened?" asked Maia as she cleaned her hands. "Where are we?"

"We're aboard the *Argo*," said Nate, "or at least what's left of it. They made few repairs."

"How did I get here?"

"Icarus flew you back after you collapsed," said Matthias. "You were bleeding badly from your leg. I'm a fool for not noticing sooner, but I was taken aback by Hephaestus and his disclosures."

"The jars. You really think they're important?"

"Yes," said Matthias. "My recollection of my final day as a Titan is hazy at best, but I don't think I'm wrong about this."

"What else did Hephaestus say about the jars?"

"Hephaestus jumped off the side of the mountain. We were all worried about you and failed to stop him."

"He jumped?"

"I guess Dorian put the idea in his head," said Nate.

"Either that or he was unsettled by our conversation."

"Dad, I'm sorry for how I spoke to you," said Maia.

"You had a sliver of hardened molten rock in your leg," said Matthias. "Between that and the bleeding, you weren't in a right state of mind."

"You really think Zeus used Pandora's jar or something like it to hold your 'godly energies' before he created Olympia?" asked Maia.

"Yes," answered Matthias. "Dorian didn't agree with me at first, but he searched Zeus's sanctuary. It is largely intact. Behind the throne, there is a row of jars crafted by Hera herself. And two appear to be missing."

"Circe came all the way to Mount Olympus to steal two jars," said Maia. "I want to believe you, but it doesn't make sense."

"Actually, it makes far more sense than you think," said Icarus as he entered the cabin. "My father will explain."

Matthias and Nate lifted Maia and helped her climb to the deck of the *Argo*. The scene before her was uninspiring at best. Though the Argonauts continued to labor, the *Argo* was in worse shape than she'd recalled. The Amazons were gathered in prayer around Io's body. Dorian was pacing, looking up every so often and shaking his head. Resting against a pile of ropes was Daedalus, his head covered in bandages. Maia limped toward him.

"What does Circe want with Pandora's jar?"

Daedalus let his head drop back. His jaw was swollen and raw. Daedalus brushed his tongue along his bottom lip and swallowed heavily.

"It is not Pandora's jar that Circe seeks. There is scarcely enough of it left for her purposes. She seeks another vessel."

"Did Zeus use Pandora's jar to create Olympia?" asked Matthias.

"In a sense," answered Daedalus. "Lord Zeus had to act quickly to separate Olympia from the homeworld, and when the time came he was not ready. He used Pandora's jar and two others like it to hold the energies released by Poseidon, Hera, and Atlas until he could forge this world."

"Is that why the fragments of Pandora's jar can be used to breach the barrier?" asked Nate.

"When I learned from King Alphaios that Lord Zeus intended to send an envoy to the homeworld, I hypothesized given the energies the jar once possessed that it could be used to do so. And I was correct."

"What does King Alphaios have to do with any of this?" asked Maia.

"Lord Zeus listened to King Alphaios, and King Alphaios listened to me," said Daedalus. "I was able to influence Lord Zeus through his so-called council. He allowed King Alphaios to take possession of Pandora's jar. I, in turn, discovered a means by which the jar could be weakened enough to break it into pieces. And you know the rest."

"Actually, I think there is much more you are not telling us," said Dorian. "You and the king had a falling out after Matthias and I journeyed to the homeworld with Hera, yet you still managed to secure some pieces of the jar for yourself."

"As did several others," said Daedalus. "You have benefited from this yourself."

"Yes, but what happened between you and King Alphaios? More than anyone else, he favored your advice. And then you were tossed aside."

"It was the witch. You invited Circe to assist you in securing new identities in the homeworld. She became embroiled in King Alphaios's affairs and soon they fell in love. Or perhaps Circe entrapped him. Either way, over time King Alphaios wanted nothing more to do with me. I took what I could of Pandora's jar, and I left his island for the last time. Eventually, Circe tired of being a wife, and she abandoned her husband and daughter to resume her wicked ways. She went underground for a time, resurfacing after King Alphaios killed himself. I suspect that Circe has been manipulating events in Olympia for quite some time."

"That's funny coming from you," said Maia.

"I admit that I sought to control the growing chaos in Olympia, but only to protect its denizens. His intentions were good, but without his wife, Lord Zeus was lost. The council led by King Alphaios only made matters worse."

"Icarus, what do you make of this?" asked Matthias.

"While my father does enjoy engaging in revisionist history to make himself appear more important, he is telling the truth for the most part."

"The other jars," said Maia. "You said there were two others. What happened to them?"

"Lord Zeus kept them in his possession."

"Until Circe claimed them," said Matthias.

"Yes, but what does it matter?" asked Nate.

"My father thinks they could be used to destroy the barrier," said Maia.

"As do I," said Daedalus.

"Would anyone else have recognized the jars for what they were?" asked Maia. "Heracles also wanted to bring down the barrier. Would he have known to take them?"

"I do not believe so," said Dorian. "He was in the Underworld when much of this transpired. But Circe would have known."

"And if Circe waited for Heracles to engineer his own downfall, she would be able to retrieve the jars from Mount Olympus," said Maia. "She *actually* has a way to destroy the barrier."

"But not the motive," said Nate.

"She's insane. What other motive does she need?" asked Maia.

"There is also her daughter," added Icarus.

"Also insane," said Maia, "and eager to have her revenge on me at all costs."

"Can it be that simple, Matthias?" asked Dorian.

"It's surprising how simple an explanation can be when you pare it down, brother," said Matthias.

"We still don't know where to find Circe and Akantha," said Nate.

"Yes, we do," said Maia. "We should've looked there to start. They're on King Alphaios's island. I'm sure of it."

Matthias clapped his hands together. "How do we get there? We thought we would find the means of returning to earth here on Mount Olympus, but that was clearly an act of hubris."

"Does anyone have some Gorgon's blood?" asked Maia.

"I am sorry, but did you ask for the blood of a Gorgon?" asked Icarus.

"Funny you should ask," said Nate.

"You are joking," said Icarus. "By no means do you have the blood of a Gorgon on board."

"We have the *aegis*, Athena's shield, and in the center of it is—"

"The head of the Gorgon Medusa!" cried Icarus.

"Poeas! Hylas! Can you bring the *aegis* up on deck?" asked Nate.

"We're lucky the Argonauts found it," said Maia.

"Yes, lucky indeed," said Dorian.

"What is the matter, brother? Do you not enjoy the sight of your former lover?" asked Matthias, stifling a laugh.

"Lover? Okay, that's gross," said Nate.

"She was not quite so... scaly when I lay with her," said Dorian.

"You mean, forced yourself on her," said Maia. "Revisionist history. Am I right, Daedalus?"

Daedalus groaned.

"I am not proud of many of my actions as a god of Olympus, including those that ultimately led to the head of Medusa being bound to that shield. Be that as it may, I do believe I understand your intentions. Were we able to siphon some blood from it, we could conceivably create a means of transportation."

"What did you do with the sliver from my leg?" asked Maia.

"It's below deck, too" said Nate. "I'll get it."

"You impress me, Maia," said Dorian. "You have always been resourceful, but you are practically bursting forth with wisdom."

"Maybe it *was* the golden apple I took from Atalanta," said Maia.

Nate ran toward the group, the sliver of hardened molten rock pressed between his thumb and forefinger. Poeas and Hylas followed with the *aegis*.

"Do you think this'll work?" asked Nate.

Maia looked to Dorian. He was rubbing his chin. After a moment, Dorian pressed his palms up.

"There is only one way to find out," said Dorian. "We must get to soil."

The group, save for Daedalus, jumped from the deck of the *Argo* to the ground below. Squinting his eyes, Nate pointed the sliver at the head of Medusa. "I'm not sure where to—"

"Give me that!" said Dorian. "If anyone should do this, it should be me."

Grimacing, Dorian thrust the sliver into Medusa's cheek. For several seconds, nothing happened.

"Maybe all the blood is dried up?"

A trickle of blood spilled down from the Gorgon's cheek and struck the ground causing it to quake.

"Stand back!" cried Dorian as a magnificent winged horse burst forth from the spot where Medusa's blood had dripped. It landed next to Queen Hippolyta. Though not as luminous as Lampus, the newly born stallion was still an impressive sight to behold.

"Mine," said the queen.

"Holy crap!" yelled Nate. "Do it again!"

Dorian stuck the head several times more, each jab yielding the same result. Soon, each member of the party had their own pterippus except for Daedalus. He was tied to his son's back after Icarus had moved his ring and retracted his wings.

"Congratulations, Dorian," said Matthias.

"For what?" asked Nate. "It was Maia's idea to use a Gorgon's blood."

"Yes, but it would not have been possible had Dorian not—"

"That is quite enough!" interrupted Dorian.

Matthias threw his head back in laughter. "Yes, well, perhaps you can pass out cigars later."

"Whoa, are these horses all Dorian's kids?" asked Nate. "That's crazy!"

"Add it to the list," said Maia.

"Are we quite done?" asked Dorian.

"Lead the way, brother," said Matthias.

"To victory!" cried Dorian as his horse reared back. The animal's wings stretched out as it dove through the clouds below.

Maia and Nate exchanged smiles.

"That list is getting pretty long," said Maia before her and Nate's horses pushed off the ground and disappeared through the clouds.

CHAPTER TWENTY-THREE

HERA'S GIFT

THE PLUNGE FROM MOUNT OLYMPUS was no less thrilling than the ascent. Maia kept a tight grip on her ebony winged stallion. She'd named him Ozzy in her head. Ahead of her, Dorian led the group past the fragments of Iris's rainbow to a murky crimson sky.

"It's gotten much worse," yelled Maia to Nate.

Nate shouted back, "I think we're running out of time. Circe must be close to demolishing the barrier."

"*Heeyah!*" cried Maia, pushing Ozzy closer to Icarus. "Is your father okay?"

Icarus laughed. "I did not expect you to worry about his health. He will be fine. I will bring him to Varkiza and then meet you on the island of King Alphaios."

"Is it much farther?" asked Maia.

"I suspect we will be back in regular space in another moment."

To Maia's right, a pterippus rode by her father swooped down alongside her. Matthias made little effort to conceal his grim expression.

"Are you alright?" he asked.

"I feel much better," answered Maia.

"That is good. Because if you don't, I would insist you join your mother in Varkiza."

"You can insist all you want, Dad, but I'm seeing this through to the end."

Matthias shook his head. "I am proud of you. I want to lock you up and throw away the key, but I am unmistakably proud of you."

The group burst through a final layer of clouds. The sea beneath them churned violently, as waves in all directions crashed into each other. The sky was a chaotic eddy of lightning and large swathes of black emptiness. In the distance, Maia could observe the source of the bedlam – the island that once belonged to King Alphaios. Above it, the sky, if one could call it that, was completely void of substance. If there was a theoretical end of the world, Maia believed this is how it would appear. And somewhere in the mix was her baby brother.

"Be prepared for anything," said Matthias. "There's no telling how quickly the barrier will fall. If we are trapped in the wake of its collapse, there may be no salvation."

The island grew larger in size, larger in fact than Maia expected or recalled.

"It doesn't look like an island. It looks like a continent," said Maia.

The air began to shake as a massive wave of energy burst forth from the island. Maia directed Ozzy to duck the jagged bolts of yellow and white that followed. Orpheus was not so fortunate. His horse nearly disintegrated upon impact with an ungodly lightning strike, sending him screaming to the sea. Dorian's horse ducked and weaved, and Maia followed suit. They were seconds away from the island. Another wave of energy charged the air around them.

"Easy boy, we're almost there," said Maia, patting Ozzy's mane.

The remains of King Alphaios's castle appeared through the trees, and Maia felt a lump in her throat. In front, there was a huge gathering of hybrids. On the castle steps stood a woman bathed in orange light. At last they'd found Circe. She didn't look as much like the wicked witch of the west as Maia expected. She was actually quite beautiful. In stark contrast, next to Circe trudged her revolting servant Aeton.

"We will dispose of the creatures," said Queen Hippolyta. "I trust you can handle the witch."

"With pleasure, your highness," said Nate.

"Together!" cried Matthias, leaping from his horse.

Dorian and Nate quickly followed, landing but a few feet from Circe. Maia hesitated, scanning the steps for Akantha and Jordi.

Circe crossed her arms and upon opening them, a blast of force knocked Matthias, Dorian and Nate off their feet. Maia circled around them and, brandishing her sword, approached Circe from behind. The witch's head turned 180 degrees. Before Maia could strike, Circe opened her mouth and a swarm of bees assaulted Ozzy. To the sound of Aeton's insane laughter, Maia jumped off the stricken horse and rolled across the top step. Her father had managed to get close to Circe, but he was quickly sent flying back to the ground.

Maia forced her knees to bend, but waves of scalding heat emanating from the ceramic jars in front of Circe kept her down. The jars were taller than her father and etched with rope-like curls that made them appear rather ordinary except for the jags of lightning that escaped from cracks in their sides.

"Fools!" cried Circe. "You are too late. At last, I have the means to remedy Zeus's folly."

Despite the pain shooting through her entire body, Maia crawled across the stone floor. Her sword lay a few feet away. Next to it was the coin necklace her grandmother had given her years ago. It'd been ripped from her neck when she fell. Maia reached for the sword until she noticed the coin was glowing. She put out her hand, and the coin broke free from its encasement and flew into her palm. Her entire body shook from the surge of power the coin unleashed. Without any impediment, Maia stood upright. Aeton charged, and Maia knocked him out cold with one punch. Stepping over Aeton, Maia rushed Circe, knocking the witch off her feet before she could counter. Maia stood over Circe and pushed her foot into the witch's chest.

"Where's my brother?"

Circe appeared genuinely bewildered. She raised her hands to conjure a spell, but Maia pushed harder, certain she heard a *crack* from Circe's chest.

Matthias raced up the steps toward Maia, as Dorian and Nate joined in with Queen Hippolyta and the Amazons disposing of the remaining hybrids.

"Answer me!" yelled Maia.

Circe's eyes flicked briefly to the back of the castle. Maia took her meaning immediately.

"Take this," said Maia, holding out the coin. "I know where Jordi is."

"I don't understand," said Matthias.

"Just take it!" yelled Maia, shoving the coin in her father's hand. The surge of power left her body, and she once again felt the raging heat coming from the jars. Matthias's body trembled as he assumed the power from the coin.

Circe attempted to push off Maia's foot, but Matthias pushed her down with his heel.

"Go," said Matthias.

Maia bounded down the steps and ran along the remains of the castle wall. A hybrid with the face of a tiger jumped at Maia, but she sliced its face open with her shield without a second thought. Maia went around to the back of the castle, nearly skidding to a stop. Several yards ahead, in front of the royal stables, stood Akantha. She was holding a sleeping Jordi.

"Not another step," said Akantha, turning her hand over to reveal a short blade.

"He has nothing to do with us, Akantha. Let him go."

"Oh, I may, but not until we have cleared up a few things."

A fracturing noise resonated through the air. The swathes of red and black in the sky grew ever larger. The fall of the barrier seemed imminent.

"There's nothing to clear up. You're insane, just like your mother, who incidentally we just defeated."

"*Ha!* Is this how you intend to retrieve your brother? By insulting me? You really are stupid."

"I'm smart enough to know that we've won," said Maia. "Give me Jordi, and I'll see that the Amazons go easy on you."

Akantha seemed to pay Maia little mind. "You saw the jars, I assume. They will rupture at any moment."

"Then you'll die."

"I do not intend to be here much longer. My mother and I are going to the mainland. We wish to be on the Acropolis when the barrier falls."

"Your mother is under my father's foot. She's not going anywhere, and neither are you."

"How well do you remember that night?" asked Akantha, looking back at the stables. "I can recall every detail."

Maia took a tentative step toward Akantha, who seemed distracted by her own thoughts.

"You were supposed to die that night. If it were not for Icarus, you would have. I was angry with myself for such a long time, especially after my father killed himself. It was right over there, at the same spot from which you and Icarus took flight, that he jumped to his death."

Maia inched closer, pleased that Akantha appeared too busy with her speech to notice.

"I should have gone to mother then, but I chose to align myself with Queen Hippolyta and her mangy viragoes. Still, I did learn to carry a sword. That is a skill that should come in handy when I am in your world. Do you think I shall like it there?"

Maia froze. Akantha was staring directly at her, her eyes narrowed.

"You're not going anywhere," said Maia. "You're going to give me my brother, and you'll then join your mother in chains."

"No, I do not think so. Instead I will throw your brother off the cliff while you deal with them," said Akantha, motioning behind her.

The stable doors splintered apart as a trio of hybrids broke free and pounced at Maia. Akantha disappeared behind the stables. Maia instinctively reached for her sword, which still lay on the castle steps. She held her shield in front of her, but was knocked down by the first of the creatures. Maia felt the heat of its breath as it bit at her. She managed to tuck her knees in and kick the beast's feet out from under it. Another of the hybrids batted at her head. She was powerless.

Twang! Twang! Twang!

The hybrids fell to the ground. Icarus swooped down on his pterippus and landed next to Maia.

"Are you alright?" asked Icarus as he pulled Maia to her feet.

"Akantha is going to throw Jordi off the cliff!"

"Go!" yelled Icarus, breaking into a run next to Maia.

They came around the stables to the sight of Akantha standing on the edge of the cliff with Jordi held over her head. He was awake and crying.

"Akantha, please don't do this! "

Next to her, Icarus slowly loaded his bow. Before he could fire an arrow, a beast emerging from the shadows of the stables knocked him down. As Icarus fell, he tossed something at Maia. It was his ring. Maia turned back to Akantha, horrified to watch her throw Jordi over the side of the cliff.

"NO!" screamed Maia as she slipped Icarus's ring onto her finger. Wings sprouted from her back, and she took flight, flying past Akantha and over the cliff. Jordi was falling toward the jagged rocks below. Maia thrust her hands out and flapped her wings as fast as she could manage.

"Please, please, let me be fast enough!"

With Jordi inches from the rocks, Maia gained a burst of speed and grabbed Jordi under his arms. Clutching her brother, Maia veered out over the water.

"I've got you, little man. I've got you."

Jordi stopped crying. He reached out and pinched Maia's nose.

"*Ow!*" said Maia.

Jordi laughed, and Maia squeezed him tighter. He was safe.

"C'mon, we have to go help someone."

Maia circled back to the island and zoomed up the wall of earth beneath the cliff. Akantha was gone, but Nate was standing next to Icarus with Maia's bloodied sword in his hand.

"Is that—"

"It's Jordi. He's okay. And I'm glad you are too, Icarus, but where's Akantha?"

"She disappeared when I was wrestling on the ground with that creature. Thankfully, Nate finished it off."

"Where's my father?"

"He and Dorian took Circe into the castle. He said whatever you gave him is making him nearly as strong as when he was a Titan."

"It's a coin from a necklace my grandmother gave me," said Maia.

"Your grandmother, Hera, queen of the gods?" asked Icarus with a smirk.

"She hasn't held that title for a while now, but she must still have some tricks up her sleeve."

Jordi blew a raspberry, and they all laughed.

"So, this is all over?" asked Nate.

"From the look of the sky, I do not believe it is over," said Icarus.

"Not to mention Akantha. She could still—"

The ground rumbled, nearly flattening the remains of the stables.

"We have to get out of here," said Nate.

"Take your ring," said Maia, pulling it off her finger. The wings disappeared. "I'll get on your horse with Nate."

They flew to the front of the castle. Jordi whooped and laughed in Maia's arms. She grinned at seeing he appeared unhurt.

"Jordi!" yelled Matthias as he came into view.

Maia glided down and held Jordi out to her father. His hands were trembling.

"My boy, my boy. Thank the gods you're okay."

Maia kissed Jordi on the back of his head. Matthias whispered, "Thank you."

"Where's Circe?" asked Nate.

"Gone," said Dorian. "The coin seemed to lose its enchantment, and she overpowered us. Akantha ran toward her, and they disappeared in a cloud of suffocating smoke."

"We have to search the island," said Icarus.

"Don't bother," said Maia. "She's not here."

"Where could she have gone?" asked Icarus.

"To the Acropolis. Akantha said they were going there to watch the barrier fall."

"Will it fall?"

"We do not know what Circe has done to the jars, but it does not appear that we can stop it," said Dorian.

"Then we go to the Acropolis," said Maia, "and even if we can't stop the barrier from being destroyed, we'll make Circe and Akantha pay for what they've done."

CHAPTER TWENTY-FOUR

THE BARRIER FALLS

MAIA KISSED JORDI ON HIS CHEEK and handed him back to her father. Jordi squealed with delight as Matthias blew a raspberry on his stomach.

"Be careful," she said, stepping away from Matthias's horse.

"I'll meet you on the Acropolis after I bring Jordi to your mother. *Heeyah!*"

Maia waited until her father and brother disappeared over the trees before mounting Icarus's horse. "How much time do you think we have?"

"There is no way of telling," said Dorian.

"We have to prepare for the worst," said Nate.

"Agreed," said Queen Hippolyta.

They mounted their pterippi and took flight. Dorian led the way over the tumultuous seas. Midway through their flight, Triton rose through the waters and threw Dorian his trident. The sea god raised his conch shell to his lips, and a gust of wind carried Maia and the others at a dizzying pace. Land soon appeared on the horizon, and Triton's gale died down.

"*Heeyah!*" cried Dorian as he led his horse down. Maia and the others followed as they neared the Acropolis of Athens. The white columns of the Parthenon were dulled by the red and black sky, but the site remained breathtaking. Passing overhead, Maia was surprised that the Acropolis seemed void of visitors.

"Where is everyone?" asked Maia.

"With the sky the way it looks, I'm sure they've taken refuge in the temples," said Nate.

"Those who still live," said Icarus. "Circe and Akantha have been on a campaign to kill or deform as many citizens of Olympia as possible."

Dorian landed his horse in the center of the site, quickly joined by the others. He held out his trident and scanned the surrounding area.

"Do you sense something?" asked Queen Hippolyta.

"I do not believe Circe is here."

"Could we have gotten here first?" asked Nate. "Actually, we have no idea how they were traveling."

"From what I saw after Akantha transformed Atalanta, they're more than capable of using magic to get around," said Maia.

Tap. Tap. Tap.

A gray-haired woman, hunched over and leaning on a gnarled wooden walking stick, had emerged from behind the Parthenon. She was wearing a black hooded robe and brought to mind an image of Snow White's wicked stepmother.

"Don't take an apple from her," whispered Nate, apparently having the same thought as Maia. "Golden or otherwise."

"Come no further," said Dorian, raising his trident.

Tap. Tap. Tap.

The old woman continued her approach, looking up and smiling a toothless grin at Maia. Dorian slammed the trident into the ground, nearly knocking them all off their feet. But the old woman didn't falter. She came within ten feet of the group and stopped, resting both hands on top of the walking stick.

"It is good to see you with your trident again, uncle," said the old woman. "You are going to need it."

"Who are you?" asked Maia.

"Who am I? I am but an old weathered woman, but in my youth I was the most attractive of all the goddesses on Mount Olympus."

"Dear Aphrodite, what has become of you?" asked Dorian, taking his niece's wrinkled hand.

"When Mount Olympus fell, so did my face," said Aphrodite with a gentle laugh. "I survived the war but at a cost."

"How did you get here?" asked Maia. "I heard you were—"

"Hiding in a cave? I was, until earlier today."

"I brought her," said Hephaestus, sitting on the steps of the Parthenon. "I did not wish for my former wife to die alone."

"You jumped off the edge of Mount Olympus," said Icarus.

"Not as smooth a ride as when Iris lived, but I managed."

"How did you know to come here?"

"I listened to their prayers," said Hephaestus, pointing to the Parthenon. "The most faithful of our followers are gathered in the city and in the temples. They know what is about to come."

"Can you stop it?" asked Nate.

"No, we are past that point. Look at the sky. We are seconds away from the fall of Olympia."

A horse whinnied, and Matthias and his steed appeared over the Parthenon. He landed next to Maia. Matthias dismounted and pulled his daughter into an embrace.

"How's Mom?"

"She's holding your brother again. How could she be anything but full of joy?"

CRACK-KOW! CRACK-KOW!

The streaks of red in the sky thinned and shrank away. In the distance, a rhythmic series of pulses came from the south – from the direction of King Alphaios's island. A suctioning sound reverberated through the site, and for a second the sky was completely devoid of all light and substance.

Dorian shouted, "This is it! Brace yourselves!"

A massive explosion of dazzling light knocked them all off their feet. Maia squinted and rubbed her eyes. A sickeningly familiar feeling coursed through her body. When she opened her eyes, her fears were confirmed. They were still on the Acropolis, but no longer alone. They were surrounded by scores of tourists in regular attire. Scattered amongst them were former denizens of Olympia. To her right, a young girl screamed at the spectacle of the pterippi. The Parthenon was still completely intact. A number of people in robes and tunics walked out of the temple to more screams. A pair of security guards came running, yelling in Greek for them to get out of a restricted area. Several of the horses reared back and took off. Hephaestus and Aphrodite disappeared into the crowd.

Chaos overtook the site, but amidst it all a pair of tourists approached Queen Hippolyta and gestured that they wanted to take a photograph with her. The queen put her arms around them and smiled. Maia became separated from her father. Icarus flew up out of the mass of people to screams of shock and dismay. He nodded his head at Maia before soaring away.

"Over here!" called Nate. He was standing next to a pterippus, petting the horse's mane in an effort to sooth it.

"This is insanity," said Maia.

"We have to get out of here," said Nate.

"Maia!" called her father. He was on a pterippus with Dorian hovering near the Parthenon.

"Come on," said Nate. He jumped on the horse and pulled Maia up. The horse reared back, scattering the crowd. Nate and Maia followed Matthias and Dorian to a clearing next to the Erechtheion.

"What's our move?" asked Maia.

"There's no sign of Circe or Akantha," said Matthias.

"I guess I shouldn't be surprised that Akantha lied."

Dorian's trident glowed bright yellow.

"Sounion," he said. "The witch and her daughter are at Cape Sounion. My son told me."

"*AAAAIIIIYYYYEEEEEH!*"

A pair of hybrids appeared on the roof of the Parthenon. A beast with the head of a wolf and another creature part man, part crocodile snarled and jumped down into the crowd of tourists.

"To arms, sisters!" cried Queen Hippolyta, diving into the mass. The queen pushed past a group led by a tour guide holding a wooden stick topped by a small rubber temple and sliced off the heads of the hybrids.

All around Maia, people shrieked and fled in terror. Circe's hybrids appeared from all corners. The Amazons and Argonauts met them at every turn. Thyra tossed a lion-headed beast at Menoetius, who sliced it across the chest. Zetes and Cyme made similar work of a pair of creatures threatening an elderly couple backed against the Temple of Athena Nike.

"Where are they all coming from?" yelled Maia, turning her head every which way.

Icarus landed in front of her. "I flew over the city. The creatures run wild not only over the Acropolis, but the streets of Athens as well. Circe must have had them stationed here in preparation for the destruction of the barrier."

"This won't end until we dispose of Circe and her daughter. Nate, you and your men must assist Queen Hippolyta and the Amazons in protecting the people of the city," said Matthias. "Maia, Dorian, and I will go to Cape Sounion."

"What would you have me do?" asked Icarus.

"Go to Varkiza. Tell the Amazons and Argonauts to expect company."

"Good luck, firecracker," said Nate with a kiss on Maia's forehead. He whistled and Augeas swooped down on a pterippus. Nate threw himself on the back of the horse, and they took flight, headed for the city.

Icarus looked at Maia with a lopsided smile. "Ahem, yes, well 'firecracker,' I too wish you luck." He spread his wings wide and took to the sky.

Suddenly, Matthias and Dorian fell to their knees.

"What's wrong?" asked Maia, rushing to their sides.

"It's... nothing," said Matthias, clutching his heart. "We must go."

Dorian forced himself to his feet. "Brother, do you suppose... "

"Anything is possible now," said Matthias.

"What are you two talking about?"

"Don't worry, Maia," said Matthias. "We're merely feeling the aftereffects of the destruction of the barrier."

"Daedalus said it was going rain fire," said Dorian.

"And in a manner it did," said Matthias.

Maia grit her teeth. "I don't like the sound of that."

"We'll worry about it after we finish off Circe."

* * *

MAIA PUSHED HER HORSE TO FLY as fast as it could. Dorian had acquired his own steed, and he was leading Maia and her father. They hugged the shoreline. The water was calmer, but no more inviting. As they neared Cape Sounion, the Temple of Poseidon came into view. Maia leaned in. Would they find Circe there?

"Do you see anything?" yelled Matthias to Dorian.

"I see my son," answered Dorian.

In the harbor beneath the Temple of Poseidon arose Triton. He blew his conch shell, and the sea parted from the beach, past a small island in the harbor and far into the distance.

"What's he doing?" asked Maia.

"He is making preparations for when the battle is won," said Dorian.

"What the hell is that supposed to mean?"

Dorian didn't have the chance to answer. A flood of energy came forth from the temple, knocking Dorian and Maia off their horses. Matthias swerved and caught Maia, but Dorian fell to the sea.

"He'll be alright," said Matthias, directing his horse to fly around the base of the rocky promontory upon which the temple rested. "Triton will see to it." They flew up the rocky cliff side and emerged on the other side of the structure. "Hang on!"

Matthias and Maia landed several yards away from the temple. Like the Parthenon, the Temple of Poseidon had been completely restored when the barrier fell. Smoke was pouring from the far side of the temple. Maia gripped her shield and sword as they advanced. A trio of hybrids, each more hideous then the next, came bounding down the steps and charged Maia and her father.

"Halt!" cried a voice from the temple. The beasts skidded to a stop. Out from the shadows stepped Circe.

"Where's your daughter?" asked Maia, her sword pointed to strike.

"Formalities first, please," said Circe. "Welcome to Sounion."

"What are you playing at, witch?" asked Matthias.

"I play at nothing. It is over. I have won."

"You have brought an end to Olympia, but this is far from over," said Matthias.

"I would have thought you would show some gratitude."

"*Aaarrggghh!*" Matthias fell to the ground, clasping the sides of his head.

"What have you done?" yelled Maia, clutching her father by the shoulders.

Circe's mouth pulled back in a mad grin. "The energies that sustained Olympia had to go somewhere."

Matthias dug his hands into the ground, causing everything to shake violently. He threw his head back and let out an agonizing scream.

"YOU WILL REGRET THIS!" boomed Matthias.

"Dad, are you—"

Matthias stood upright and peered at his daughter. His eyes were as black as coal. Maia recoiled as the meaning of Circe's words came to her. Once again, her father possessed the might of a Titan. Matthias was no more. He was Atlas.

CHAPTER TWENTY-FIVE

ALL THAT REMAINS

THE COLUMNS OF THE TEMPLE OF POSEIDON buckled as Atlas raised his fists and screamed.

"*AAARRGGGHH!*"

Maia reached out her hand, but quickly withdrew it as her father continued to bellow. He was suffering pain so excruciating that Maia experienced it with him. She turned to Circe. The witch was smiling as she pet one of her hybrids, a man with the upper body of an ape. The remaining pair of hybrids circled their mistress, growling and drooling. They were equal parts human and panther.

"What troubles you, girl? Are you not impressed by your father?" asked Circe.

"*AAARRGGGHH!*"

Atlas fell to his knees, hammering the ground with blow after blow. He wrenched an enormous ball of dirt and rock and held it over his head. Atlas steadied himself and threw the mass at the Temple of Poseidon, demolishing a row of columns.

"Such a shame. The temple looked lovely," said Circe.

"Dad!" cried Maia. "You have to control this. We have to get back to Mom and Jordi."

"There is no returning from this, girl. If he survives, Atlas will take his place amongst the deities, not at your mother's side. Your perfect little family is no more."

Maia squeezed the hilt of her sword. Circe was lying. She had to be. But her father was in agony, stomping about and yanking his hair.

The ground shook, and Maia looked toward the remains of the temple. A jet of water gushed over the broken columns. Dorian landed in front of Maia, his trident pointed at Atlas.

"Please don't hurt him. He's not—"

Dorian jabbed Maia's shoulder with the trident, catching the corner of her tunic. He lifted her and threw her in the air. Maia spun and landed on her shield. She skidded to a stop. Dorian had been transformed as well. He was Poseidon, god of the sea.

"You dare desecrate my temple, Titan," bellowed Poseidon. "You shall pay!" He dug his trident into the ground, creating a fissure that wound its way between Atlas's legs. A surge of water erupted from the cracked soil, nearly knocking the Titan off his feet.

Atlas charged at Poseidon, leaping into the air and striking at the sea god with his fingers knotted. Poseidon stabbed Atlas in the chest, but the trident failed to penetrate his skin. Atlas landed on top of Poseidon and pummeled him with both hands. Poseidon's trident glowed, and a fist-shaped funnel of water came up from the sea and struck Atlas. He was met with several blows in rapid succession, knocking him into an olive grove. Atlas ripped a tree from its roots and hurled it at Poseidon, who knocked it aside with his trident.

"You are no match for me, Titan!" boomed Poseidon.

"We shall see, godling," yelled Atlas in turn, charging the sea god.

Atlas and Poseidon landed punch after punch. Atlas kicked Poseidon in the stomach, causing him to drop the trident. Beneath them, the sea was in turmoil. The sky crackled with lightning as rain tore down like bullets. Maia raised her shield to block the rain, trying to spot Circe. The witch was gone. Maia headed for the temple, keeping an eye open for the hybrids. Forewarn by a guttural growl, she spun around and sliced a panther hybrid across its chest. Maia paused to wipe a spray of blood from her chin when the gorilla hybrid pounced. She knocked it aside with her shield and somersaulted over the beast, driving her sword in its neck. One more, Maia thought.

"*AAARRGGGHH!*"

Atlas and Poseidon continued their assault on each other. Maia ran for the temple steps. The roof had collapsed after Atlas's initial attack, but she was partially protected from the torrential rain. Maia moved further into the structure. A statue of Poseidon had been toppled and lay in pieces. A thundering crash sounded to her right, as Poseidon himself fell through the remains of the roof and knocked over a pair of columns. Maia sprinted past the altar and out of the temple, stopping at the cliff's edge. The rain continued in droves. Poseidon rose up and leaped at Atlas, the two deities trading hits. The earth shook with their combat, and hunks of the cliff broke off and fell to the sea.

"We have to stop meeting like this," said a familiar voice. Akantha stood next to the remaining panther hybrid. Circe's daughter was wearing the armor of an Amazon and bore a matching shield and sword.

"You don't deserve to wear that armor," said Maia.

"And you do? Who in Hades are you?"

"Who am I?" Maia cut a figure eight in the space between them with her sword. "I'm Maia, daughter of Eleanor and Matthias, and Jordi's big sister. I'm a child of two worlds. And, unlike you, I'm an Amazon."

"Nonsense! A couple of days going rounds with Penelopeia, and – *poof!* – you were made an Amazon," said Akantha. "I trained for years. And I daresay I am prepared to end your life this time."

"Where's your mother?"

"Where is yours? I am certain you believe her to be safe, clasping your precious baby brother to her breast, but I assure you that no one you love will escape this unharmed."

"And what is this exactly?" asked Maia. "What purpose did destroying the barrier serve?"

"*Humph!* Because I desired it to fall and to bring you pain and suffering."

Maia lowered her sword. "So that's really it, then? I know I've said it before, but you're insane. You are truly 100% crazy. All of this, everything you and your mother have created is pure chaos. What do you think is going to happen once you've killed me? You're going to take over the world by snapping your fingers? Olympia was a fraction of the size of the earth, and you couldn't rule there."

"I do not have to rule the entire world."

"But that's just it. You'll have the rest of the countries to contend with. You've been so blinded with hatred and thoughts of revenge that you've set up your own defeat. Can't you see that?" asked Maia.

"I see everything!" cried Akantha.

"Apparently not," said Maia, backing away.

"What are you—"

Atlas and Poseidon landed just two feet away from Akantha. The ground fractured, and the deities fell through the earth as it gave way. The panther hybrid wailed as it fell to the sea below. Akantha scrambled to avoid the same fate, but she disappeared in a cloud of dust. Maia rushed to the side of the cliff, careful to avoid the unstable rocks. She couldn't see past the edge. Maia turned and ran toward the road. She had only noticed the rain had stopped when a shield struck her from behind. The weapon hit her below her waist, and she fell on her face. Her sword and shield flew from her hands. Rolling over, she witnessed Akantha pull herself up from the edge of the cliff. Akantha wiped blood from the corner of her mouth.

"Going somewhere?"

Maia shook her head as she retrieved her sword and shield. Stretching her back, she walked toward Akantha's shield and kicked it off the side of the cliff.

"Oops."

"No matter," said Akantha. "I do not need a shield to best you."

"Neither do I," said Maia, dropping her shield to the ground.

Akantha rushed forward, her sword leveled at Maia. Stepping back, Maia blocked the strike, sparks flying from where their swords made contact. Akantha pushed forward and their swords met at their hilts. Maia broke away and spun around. Akantha swung wildly, stumbling forward. She turned and scowled at Maia. They circled one another. Akantha dashed across the rocky terrain, and their swords met again. Faster and faster, they counteracted each other. Akantha gained the advantage, but lost it immediately to Maia who backed Akantha up to the remains of the cliff.

"Hell of a way to go," said Maia.

Akantha knocked Maia's sword aside and stepped around her, pointing her sword at Maia's chest.

"Yes, it would be," said Akantha.

They continued to trade strikes, keeping each other close to the edge. Akantha rushed forward in a frenzy, and Maia slashed her arm.

"Aiyeeh!"

Akantha spun around, but the dirt beneath her gave way. She fell to her knees. Akantha raised her sword to block an attack by Maia, but Maia kicked Akantha's sword from her hands.

With her sword aimed at Akantha's neck, Maia said, "It's over."

Akantha lowered her head, sobbing. Maia stepped back and raised an eyebrow. Akantha moved to pull a pouch from her belt, and Maia severed her hand. The pouch fell to the ground, and a spray of mustard-yellow powder struck Akantha in the face.

"NOOOOO!" Akantha bawled as she fell forward.

Maia stepped away from Akantha as she writhed on the floor. She raised her sword to end Akantha's misery, but thought better of getting close to the powder. Akantha's screams became higher and higher culminating in a protracted squeal. Her legs twisted together into an elongated tail, and her skin morphed into bright red scales. Akantha – now part amphisbaena – lifted her head. Her eyes were narrow, and a thin forked tongue darted out of her mouth.

"Hiiiiiiisssssss!"

Akantha rose up on her tail. The scales at the end of the tail boiled, and a second head burst forth. The first head sniped at the second as the former princess twisted across the terrain. Maia took several short steps and picked up her shield. In the midst of her transformation, Akantha didn't seem to notice her.

Once she was several feet away, Maia darted for the road. As she passed the remains of the temple, she feared for what had become of Atlas and Poseidon.

"Hiiiiiiisssssss!"

The beast slithered around the columns and lunged at Maia with its fangs. She blocked one head with her shield, while stabbing at the second. The head at the end of its tail screeched as the other jabbed at Maia. She stumbled, but regained her footing. Maia rotated her core, slicing the beast across the fragments of its armor. With the backswing, she sliced off both heads. The beast crashed to the ground. Maia raised her sword and brought it down into Akantha's chest for the final blow.

Gasping for air, Maia dropped to one knee. She bowed her head and closed her eyes. Akantha was no more.

"So senseless," whispered Maia.

Moments later, Maia heard the sound of crushing gravel. A car was pulling up to the site. Maia stood, completely at a loss how to explain her circumstances.

"Where is he?" yelled a man running toward her. It was Apolyn. "Where is Dorian?"

Maia ran her tongue over her cracked bottom lip. "He fell off the side… with my father… but they weren't themselves."

"Well, I figured that after your grandmother disappeared. *Ugh!* Okay, get in!"

Maia caught up with Apolyn as he slid into the driver's seat. Closing the car door behind her, Maia asked, "What do you mean my grandmother disappeared?"

Apolyn shifted into reverse and pivoted the car around, nearly hitting a pterippus.

"Yours, I assume?"

"I thought they flew away when the fighting started," said Maia. This was going to take some adjustment.

Maia leaned her head back as Apolyn sped down the winding road. The car skidded to a stop, and Apolyn jumped out. He ran down to the surf and put his hand in the water.

"What are you doing?" asked Maia.

Out in the harbor, a cone of water broke the surface of the water. At its core was Atlas, spinning endlessly at the mercy of

Poseidon, who was floating at the head of the cone. Atlas escaped from the funnel and landed on top of Poseidon. They disappeared under the water for mere seconds before Poseidon came flying out backwards. Flipping in the air, he splashed back under the water.

"How are we going to stop them?" asked Maia.

"Fear not, child," came a voice from above.

A woman in a billowing gown of the purest white Maia had ever seen hovered over them. She smiled at Maia.

"Hera will take care of her boys."

CHAPTER TWENTY-SIX

THE ISLAND

HERA, QUEEN OF THE GODS OF OLYMPUS, touched down at the water's edge, the surf parting beneath her sandals of gold. Maia shielded her eyes from the warm, dazzling glow the goddess emitted. Of all the odd things Maia had been witness to in Olympia, her grandmother's resumption of immortality was amongst the most surprising. Hera turned and gazed upon Maia.

"You have done well, child."

"Thank you, but Circe got away."

"One thing at a time," said Hera as the corners of her mouth pulled back.

Maia's face reddened. Hera was as beautiful as she was commanding.

"Triton, may I have your assistance?" called Hera. Her voice echoed through the harbor.

Several yards out, Triton rose up from the water. He nodded at Hera and brought his conch shell to his lips.

BAAAAAAAOOOOOOOOOOOO!

A path materialized in front of Hera bordered by walls of rushing water. The sandy passageway extended far into the harbor, creating an arena.

Splash!

Breaking through the wall of water, Atlas and Poseidon fell into the arena. The sea god had Maia's father in a chokehold with his trident.

"YIELD!" cried Poseidon.

"NE – *cough, cough!* – VER!"

"They really are children," said Hera, gliding down the path.

Maia laughed into her hand. It was almost too much to take. She scurried behind Hera.

"BOYS! BOYS!" called Hera. "That is quite enough."

Atlas and Poseidon looked at Hera in unison, their eyes betraying their shock and embarrassment. Poseidon released Atlas from his hold. With a quick elbow to Poseidon's stomach, Atlas rolled back and jumped to his feet. Poseidon doubled over, then drove his trident into the sand and stood next to Atlas.

"If you are finished with your strutting, there is much work to be done," said Hera.

"Forgive me, sister," said Poseidon, "but such madness overtook me when my godly energies returned."

"I also felt this madness," said Atlas. "Were you also affected?"

"No."

"And why is that, sister?" asked Poseidon, pulling his shoulders back.

"Because the female gender has always been stronger," said Hera, winking at Maia.

"Maia!" cried Atlas, reaching out his hand. "Are you injured?"

"I'm okay," said Maia, "but what about you?"

Atlas shrugged. "The sea god is far from the most challenging opponent I have faced."

"I daresay, 'brother,' I would be keen to go another round," said Poseidon, thrusting his trident down farther in the sand.

"Dad, what I meant was, are you going to be able to come home like that? You're a... "

"Titan. Yes, I take your meaning. I can hardly go back to your mother in this form. I am sorry, Maia, but I did not expect the fall of Olympia to have such consequences."

"Nor did I," said Poseidon, looking past Maia. Apolyn stood on the beach, his face showing little emotion.

"Isn't there anything we can do?" asked Maia, her eyes falling upon Hera.

"Indeed, there is much we must do. The Amazons and Argonauts have been cast over all of Greece, destroying Circe's remaining beasts. But the witch's hybrids are far from the only creatures that need to be gathered. We cannot have satyrs and Cyclopes roaming the countryside."

"And what would you have us do, sister?" asked Poseidon. "Recreate Olympia?"

"No, that would be impossible, even if we three were to relinquish our energies. Yet there is a suitable alternative. When the barrier fell, the island of King Alphaios was carried here. It is unpopulated by man. We will collect the remaining denizens of Olympia and every other non-native living thing and bring them to the island."

"Impossible!" cried Poseidon. "Such folly is outweighed only by Zeus's original plan."

"I think Dorian, I mean, Poseidon is right. I can only imagine what's going on all over Greece. The people must be terrified. I'm surprised the government hasn't sent in the military. How can we transport everyone and everything to the island without causing a panic?"

"Leave that to me, child, and to my 'boys,' of course."

"You are my sister, Hera."

"And technically, I am uncle to both of you," said Atlas.

"No sense of humor," said Hera, looking at Maia.

"I grow tired of this," said Poseidon.

"If you are willing to relinquish your energies, I can use them to cast an enchantment over Greece to undo whatever damage has already been wrought. Once we have gathered them along the shores, Triton will create additional passages to the island for its new occupants. I will use the remaining energies to create a protective barrier over the island. No one will enter or exit without permission."

"Whose permission?" asked Atlas.

"Mine," answered Hera, a weak smile forming.

"Do you wish to be guardian of the island?" asked Poseidon.

"I do not," said Hera, "but I lived a favorable life as a mortal. And I do not have loved ones to return to as you do."

"That's not true," said Maia, her lip quivering.

"Thank you, child," said Hera. "I care for you as well, and I hope you will visit the island."

"Of course!"

"Well, then it is settled," said Poseidon.

"I have a question for you, Hera," said Atlas. "Who is going to tell Queen Hippolyta that she has to go live on the island?"

* * *

MAIA STOOD ON THE PROMONTORY of Cape Sounion, the Temple of Poseidon behind her. From this vantage point, she could see several of Triton's paths extending out to the island of King Alphaios. The litany of travelers could fill the glossary of a book of Greek mythology. A trio of Amazons led a muzzled chimera down the path, followed by a herd of a bull with bushy fur called a catoblepas. Hyena-like crocotta scurried along the seawall. Scores of Amazons and Argonauts guarded the paths, ensuring minimal conflict.

"*Heeyah!*"

Nate flew past Maia on a pterippus. He came around and landed a few feet away. Nate dismounted the horse and sidled up to Maia.

"The boy Orion and his father arrived safely on the island," said Nate.

"Thank you for checking," said Maia, putting her arm around Nate's waist. "Do you think it's going to work?"

"Your guess is as good as mine. But I have faith in Hera. I'm not sure why I have faith in her, but I do," said Nate, chuckling.

"I do, too."

Noise of a scuffle came from the path leading from the beach below. Captain Penelopeia jumped between a satyr and a nymph, aiming her sword at the satyr's crotch.

"The Amazons are going to have their hands full," said Nate.

"Queen Hippolyta said they're happy to have a home," said Maia. "It seems crazy, but everyone seems so easy going about the whole thing."

"What choice do they have?"

"I suppose," said Maia, her eyes lingering on the Temple of Poseidon. After the fight between Atlas and Poseidon, it was in just as much a ruined state as it was before the barrier fell. But the columns weren't aged. "There's going to be a lot of confusion when Hera drops her spell, and the people of Greece wake up to their 'ruins' looking unaffected by the passage of time."

"I think it's going to be awesome. There should be some magic in the world."

"And what about you?" asked Maia.

"What about me?"

"Are you going back to the United States?"

Nate took hold of Maia's hands. "Eventually, I will. But first I'm going to spend some time on the island helping everyone get settled."

"Your father would be proud," said Maia.

"I hope so," said Nate. "Have you thought about what you're going to do?"

"First thing I'm going to do is go play blocks with Jordi. After that, I have no idea."

"Maybe a shower?"

Maia punched Nate in the stomach.

"*Ooof!* Remind me not to joke around with any of the Amazons on the island," said Nate, rubbing his stomach.

"I especially wouldn't pull that crap with Captain Penelopeia."

* * *

MAIA PASSED THROUGH THE SLIDING GLASS DOORS of the Laiko General Hospital of Athens. She walked down a sloping sidewalk to a bench where her mother sat with Jordi fidgeting on her lap.

"How's Helena?" asked Eleanor, extracting Jordi's finger from her ear.

"She seems okay," said Maia. "She was going on about how cute one of the doctors is, so I guess she's on the mend."

"What's that about?"

"I don't know. Sometimes I think there's a lot more to Helena than just chasing guys, but then maybe that's just her."

"Not every woman is going to be an Amazon, and that's acceptable," said Eleanor.

Maia grinned as she sat next to her mother. "You don't need to carry a sword and shield to be a badass."

"Does that mean you've decided to come home?" asked Eleanor, averting her eyes.

"Yeah," said Maia, scooping Jordi onto her lap. "But if it's okay with you and Dad, I'd like to travel around Greece with Dorian and Apolyn. I want to see what's new. And then maybe I'll meet up with Jackie in Spain."

"Sounds like you have it all figured out," said Eleanor.

"I'll be home before the end of the summer. I just need some time."

"You can take all the time you need, sweetie. Believe me, I need some, too."

A shadow cast across Maia's feet, and someone appeared in front of her blocking the afternoon sun.

"Forgive me for intruding," said Icarus. "Matthias brought me. He is waiting for you at the bottom of the hill."

"Thank you, Icarus," said Eleanor, taking Jordi from Maia. "Do you guys need a minute?"

"I'll see you at the house," said Maia.

"Okay, but no flying."

"You have my word," said Icarus, bowing.

Maia watched her mother and brother stroll down the hill to her waiting father. Jordi waved and blew raspberries.

"How are things on the island?" asked Maia.

"My father has angered quite a few people so far."

"He must be feeling better."

"Yes, sadly, he is back to his old self," said Icarus. "Other than that, the island is truly a wondrous place."

"Wondrous, eh?"

"Poor choice of a word?"

"No, it's perfect," said Maia, pulling Icarus into an embrace.

Icarus stiffened for a moment and then returned the hug. "I will miss you."

"Don't let your wife hear that."

Icarus smiled that same dopey grin that both irritated and intrigued Maia all those years ago. "My wife is pregnant."

"Congratulations!" said Maia, squeezing Icarus even tighter.

"I hope I will be a better father than my own."

"There's no doubt about that."

Icarus nodded his head. "May I ask you something, Maia? Are you pleased with how things turned out?"

"That's a complicated question."

"Do you feel the same as you did when we spoke on the beach in Varkiza?"

"Well, my parents are back together. And I have a little brother. So, I guess I am pleased."

"You are also an Amazon. But more than that, you are a hero worthy of standing alongside the mightiest champions of Olympus."

"Does that mean I've completed my hero's journey?"

"That is entirely up to you."

"*Hmmm.* I think I'm going to hang up my shield and just enjoy being eighteen for a while."

"Then, I hope you are truly happy."

"For the first time in a long time, I am. And I have you to thank, I suppose. If you hadn't shot me with that arrow, maybe I never would've gotten my father back."

"Along with everything else, you have acquired a great sense of perspective."

"I imagine flying will do that."

CHAPTER TWENTY-SEVEN

THE CHOICE

VARKIZA BEACH WAS EMPTY except for Maia and her father, a far cry from when Maia was last there. She'd taken her father's hand at some point, intentionally but as casually as possible. Her father smiled at her as they reached the end of the wooden board-walk and stepped onto the sand. They walked to the water's edge and sat. Maia leaned in and rested her head on her father's arm.

"What is it, Maia?"

"Back on Sounion, I thought I lost you again," said Maia, biting her lip. "What was it like?"

"Poseidon described it best when he called it 'madness.' I was not prepared for the power I once held."

"Were you tempted to keep it?"

"Not even for a second. I was pleased that Hera was able to formulate a plan that required me to embrace mortality. I could not bear to be apart from you and mother and brother."

Maia squinted and stared out at the sea. "What do you think is happening on the island?"

"I'm certain that Queen Hippolyta has things well in hand. She has your sister Amazons. And Nate and the Argonauts. Do you wish to visit before you leave?"

Maia thought for a moment and shook her head.

"I'm not ready for that."

"I understand. I crave the normalcy of home and work."

"Normalcy has been in pretty short demand," said Maia.

"Which makes me cherish it even more," said Matthias. "I'm glad you're going to spend some time here after we leave. The whole of Greece has changed."

"Circe is still out there."

"She won't elude capture for long. Whatever spells she's using to conceal herself won't sustain."

"Do you think she knows I killed Akantha?" asked Maia.

"You did not kill Akantha. She was responsible for her own death."

"Yeah, but I—"

"Akantha and her mother set the events in motion that led to her transformation. If anything, you merely ended her suffering," said Matthias.

"I doubt Circe would see it that way."

"Circe is likely huddled in a cave, cold and hungry. And when she reveals herself, she will be brought to justice."

Maia and her father sat in silence. A glint of light came off Maia's bracelet, her gift from Zeus. Maia turned the bracelet until she came upon the symbol of the amphisbaena.

"Why do you think this symbol appeared when we were back home?" asked Maia.

"I think the only one who knows the answer to that is Zeus."

"I can't ask him."

"Perhaps when Akantha struck at you using the book, the bracelet predicted her fate," said Matthias.

"That sounds crazy," said Maia.

"Can you truly categorize anything as *crazy* anymore?"

"I guess not."

"Well, I'm going to return to your mother and brother," said Matthias. "I'm sure Dorian and Apolyn have more to do than serve as bodyguards."

"I'm going to stay for a little while."

Matthias kissed Maia on top of her head. His feet made a squishing sound as he walked up the beach. Maia stretched out her legs and put her feet in the water. A moment passed, and a tear rolled down Maia's cheek. She wiped her chin with the back of her hand.

Despite her father's reassurances, it pained Maia to think of Akantha's death. Yes, the former princess was a hateful, vengeful brute, but she was, like Maia, a victim of circumstances. Not unlike all of the inhabitants of Olympia. She thought about the boy Orion and wondered how he was adjusting to his new home. Maia thought about Nate and imagined him coping with all of the fantastic creatures now populating the island. She also thought about being with him and seeing where their relationship may go.

But first, she would travel Greece with Dorian and Apolyn. And then she would meet up with Jackie and Roc in Spain.

And what about after that?

College?

The island?

A rock shifted next to Maia's hand. A spider crawled out from beneath and scurried to the surf. A wave came and washed the spider out into the water. Maia had never seen a spider at the beach before.

"Surrounded, detached, in measureless oceans of space," she murmured.

Maia grinned as an image entered her mind – Memorial Park in Sea Cliff. Hopefully, her favorite bench had been fixed. After Spain, she'd go home to Sea Cliff, she'd decided. Perhaps she'd sit in Memorial Park with her guitar and write a ballad about the fall of Olympia. Or she could bring Jordi there to play hide and seek.

Or maybe she'd wait for someone else to do something stupid and take up Jackie's suggestion to be a superhero.

The choice of journey was hers alone to make, and the possibilities were endless.

EPILOGUE I

WHEN ELEANOR WENT HOME

I HAD TO GET OUT OF THAT HOUSE. I know my parents mean well, but if they wanted to ensure my welcome home wasn't completely smothering, they wouldn't have invited all of their friends.

Thank goodness Maia started crying and gave me an excuse to take her for a walk. There's a place I've wanted to show her since we got in last night, and it's just a couple of blocks away.

I turn onto Prospect Avenue, and it hits me like a ton of bricks. I'm back home. Greece and Matt's family are half a world away. And Matt? Well, who knows where he is. I have to think about Maia. She's all that matters now.

I'm pleasantly surprised to find Memorial Park is empty. I cross the street and push Maia's stroller onto the sidewalk. Entering the park, I follow the crescent-shaped path to the bench in the middle of the park.

Maia is still asleep, so I push her stroller next to the bench and sit down. The view is as stunning as I remember. There's nothing but water for the eye to see.

My stomach turns as it hits me how much the view reminds me of Cape Sounion. Matt took me there on the day we met. And we were married there.

Matt teased me for months about what I thought I saw out in the water on the day we were married. I swore there was a man with a long white beard holding a conch shell, just floating on the surface. Matt said the gods of Olympus had sent the god of the sea to bless our wedding. For all the good it did us.

Maia stirs, and I pull back her blanket. She's cooing in her sleep. I stroke her palm, and she grabs my finger.

"We're going to be okay, Maia."

The sky darkens, and I unlock the back wheels on Maia's stroller and push her down the path. I look out to the water one last time, and there's a man out in the water with a long white beard holding a conch shell. I blink, and the man disappears.

"I think I need to take a nap, too."

I exit the park and begin the short walk back to my parents' house.

"Yes, everything is going to be okay."

EPILOGUE II

ONE DAY AFTER THE DESTRUCTION OF OLYMPIA

STANDING IN HER NEWLY CRAFTED TEMPLE, Hera, queen of the gods, looked upon her scrying pool. Things were going well on the island. Queen Hippolyta and her Amazons had begun the process of finding shelter for the survivors of Olympia. Jason's son and the Argonauts had successfully confined most of the creatures to the woods, an incantation placed upon them to prevent them from leaving. Nymphs had taken up residence in streams and meadows. The Cyclopes had staggered their way to the far side of the island, taking refuge in the mountains. Scores of pterippi made their home in the sky.

Hera was pleased. But she was also alone. Aphrodite and Hephaestus had ventured to the island but refused to return to Mount Olympus. Hades, god of the Underworld, had not yet made himself known.

"Lord Zeus, if only you could have seen this."

The space above Mount Olympus echoed with a clap of thunder, and an icy breeze winded through the columns of the temple. From a blazing flash of light emerged a figure in robes.

"Greetings, wife," said Zeus, king of the gods.

Hera covered her mouth with her hand. "How is this possible, husband?"

"A contingency should anything befall Olympia."

"You gave of your godly energies as well?"

"A trifle. Nothing like the sacrifice you made. But enough force, when released, to bring your husband back."

"Look upon the scrying pool," said Hera. "Olympia lives on."

Zeus positioned himself beside his wife. "I am very impressed. You are a most capable leader."

"I turn Mount Olympus back over to you, husband."

"And I refuse it, unless you intend to share the throne with me as my equal."

Hera took her husband's hand. "You are full of surprises."

"Dear wife, you have not seen anything yet."

The End

APPENDIX

PEOPLE, PLACES & THINGS

ACROPOLIS – an ancient fortress in the city of Athens containing the ruins of several buildings, including the Parthenon, the Erechtheion, and the Temple of Athena Nike

ACHAEANS – a collective name for the Greeks who fought during the Trojan War

AEGIS – the shield of Athena, bearing the head of the Gorgon Medusa

AEGLE – a nymph of the West and caretaker of the garden of the Hesperides

AKANTHA – the daughter of King Alphaios; taken in by the Amazons after his death; from the Greek word for "thorn" (o)

ALALA – a Greek battle cry; the daughter of Polemos

ALPHAIOS – a Greek king and the father of Akantha; former leader of a council to Zeus; took his life after being renounced by Zeus; from the Greek word for "changing" (o)

AMAZONS – a Greek tribe of mighty female warriors

AMPHISBAENA – a venomous, two-headed snake-like creature

APHRODITE – the Greek goddess of love and beauty

APOLLO – the Greek god of the sun

ARACHNE – a great weaver; transformed into a spider by the goddess Athena after beating her in a weaving contest

ARGO – the ship on which Jason and the Argonauts sailed across Greece to retrieve the Golden Fleece

ARGONAUTS – a band of heroes who accompanied Jason on his quest to find the Golden Fleece

ATALANTA – a fierce huntress; agreed to marry Hippomenes after he defeated her in a footrace

ATHENA – the goddess of wisdom and war

ATLAS – the Titan god of endurance and astronomy; father of the Pleiades and the nymphs of the West

AUTOLYCUS – a renowned Greek thief and trickster

CAPE SOUNION, GREECE – a promontory outside the city of Athens; location of the Temple of Poseidon

CATOBLEPAS – a bull with a heavy mane, bloodshot eyes, and a scaly back; its breath turned people to stone

CHARON – the ferryman of Hades who carried the dead to the Underworld

CHIMERA – a three-headed, fire-breathing creature made up of various animals

CIRCE – a Greek witch known for transforming her enemies into animals

COMUS – the Greek god of festivity and anarchy

CRETE – the largest of the Greek islands

CROCOTTA – a deadly hyena-like beast

CYCLOPS – a giant with a single eye in the middle of its forehead

DAEDALUS – a skilled craftsman and artist; father of Icarus; creator of the labyrinth on Crete

DIONYSUS – the god of wine, religious ecstasy, and ritual madness

DORIAN TRIBE – a Greek tribe founded by the hero Doros; from the Greek "Dorios," meaning "child of the sea"

EOS – the Greek goddess of the dawn who opened the gates of heaven each morning

ERIS – the goddess of strife and discord

EURYSTHEUS – a Greek king who forced twelve labours upon Heracles

GAIA – the Greek mother goddess and personification of the Earth; mother of the Titans

GARDEN OF THE HESPERIDES – Hera's orchard in which were grown golden apples that granted immortality

GODS OF OLYMPUS – the twelve major gods of ancient Greece

GOLDEN FLEECE – a coat made of wool from the golden winged ram Chrysomallos; hung on a sacred oak tree and guarded by a never-sleeping dragon

GRYPHON – a creature with the body of a lion and head and wings of an eagle

HADES – the Greek god of the Underworld

HARPY – a bird with the head of a woman, long boney claws, and a protruding stomach

HELIOS – the Greek personification of the sun

HEPHAESTUS – the Greek god of fire and metalworking

HERA – the Greek goddess of marriage and women; wife of Zeus; queen of the gods of Olympus

HERACLES – the demi-god son of Zeus and Alcmene

HIPPOLYTA – the queen of the Amazons

HIPPOMENES – a suitor of Atalanta; turned into a lion by the goddess Cybele

HOMEWORLD – a term used by denizens of Olympia to refer to Earth (o)

JASON – the rightful king of the city of Iolcos; leader of the Argonauts on their quest for the Golden Fleece; husband of Medea

ICARUS – the son of Daedalus; known as "The boy who flew too close to the sun"

IRIS – the goddess of the rainbow and messenger of the gods

KALLISTE – a daughter of the sea god Triton

KRESTENA, GREECE – a town near the site of Olympia

LABOURS OF HERACLES – twelve tasks imposed upon Heracles as penance for killing his wife and children in a fit of madness

LADON – a massive serpentine dragon that guarded the garden of the Hesperides

LAMPUS – one of two horses that pulled the chariot of Eos across the arc of heaven

MEDUSA – a winged female monster with living snakes in place of hair; her gaze turned people to stone

MOUNT OLYMPUS – the home of the gods of Greek mythology

NYMPHS OF THE WEST – female nature deities who tended the garden of the Hesperides; daughters of Atlas and Hesperius

OLYMPIA, GREECE – the site of the ancient Olympic games

OLYMPIA – a hidden world ruled by Zeus and the gods of Olympus populated by persons and creatures from Greek mythology (o)

ORPHEUS – a musician, poet, and member of the Argonauts

PALLAS – a daughter of the sea god Triton; accidentally killed by Athena due to Zeus's trickery

PAN – the Greek god of nature and the wild

PANDORA'S JAR – a large jar (often mislabeled a box) that contained all the evils of the world

PENTHESILEA – an Amazon who died fighting in the Trojan War

PLEIADES – the seven daughters of Atlas and Pleione, the eldest of whom was named Maia; transformed into stars by Zeus

POLEMOS - the Greek personification of war

POLYPHEMUS – a Cyclops and son of Poseidon

POSEIDON – the Greek god of the sea

PTERIPPI – winged horses; the offspring of Poseidon and Medusa

SATYR – a half-man, half-goat creature

SCRYING POOL – a bowl of liquid used for divination or fortune-telling

SEA CLIFF, NEW YORK – a seaside village on the north shore of Long Island

SISYPHUS – the king of Ephyra; punished by Zeus for his trickery by having to roll a boulder endlessly up a steep hill

TARTURUS – a deep abyss used as a dungeon and prison for the Titans

TITANOMACHY – a ten-year battle between the gods of Olympus and the Titans for control of the universe

TITANS – ancient Greek deities who preceded the gods of Olympus

TRITON – a Greek sea god; the son of Poseidon

TROJAN WAR – a great war waged against the city of Troy by the Achaeans

UNDERWORLD – the Greek otherworld where souls go after death; the realm of Hades

VARKIZA, GREECE – a seaside village outside the city of Athens

ZEUS – the Greek god of the sky and thunder; husband of Hera; father of Heracles; king of the gods of Olympus

(o) Denotes original concept

MAIA'S ADVENTURES
IN OLYMPIA BEGAN IN...

MAIA *and* ICARUS

When a fire destroys her home, Maia Peterson discovers a family secret that sends her halfway across the globe to Greece. Once there, Maia is whisked away to Olympia, a hidden world of creatures and characters from Greek mythology. And in this land out of time, Maia finds herself at the center of an age-old conflict between feuding gods.

MAIA *and* HIPPOLYTA

Three years after discovering a startling truth about her heritage, Maia Peterson thought it was safe to return to Olympia if she wore the magic bracelet given to her by Zeus, lord of the gods. But when the queen of the Amazons, a tribe of powerful warrior women, falls prey to a mad, bloodthirsty demi-god, Maia risks Zeus's protection to fulfill a promise once made by her long-missing father.

For more information, visit:
barrowcourtbooks.com

ACKNOWLEDGMENTS

MY SINCERE THANKS to everyone who supported the writing of *Maia and Atlas*, and especially to the many amazing readers I've met at book fairs across Long Island, including students from Stewart School in Garden City, Thomas J. Lahey School in Greenlawn, and R.J.O. Intermediate School in Kings Park.

ABOUT *the* AUTHOR

JAMES A. PEREZ has worked in the field of education for over twenty years with children of all ages. He is a proud husband, father, and lifelong comic book fan who lives on Long Island with his family.

In addition to *Maia and Icarus, Maia and Hippolyta,* and *Maia and Atlas,* he wrote *Grandpa's Walking Stick,* a picture book for his daughter, Ellie.

www.ingramcontent.com/pod-product-compliance
Lightning Source LLC
Chambersburg PA
CBHW050024180626
46810CB00002B/560